Just Another Teenage Girl

notionpress
.com

Just Another Teenage Girl

ISHA NAGAPPAN

notionpress
.com

Notion Press

Old No. 38, New No. 6
McNichols Road, Chetpet
Chennai - 600 031

First Published by Notion Press 2016

ISBN 978-93-5206-859-3

"Every teenager dreams of writing a book. Here's one bright teenager who has written not one , but two books! Isha Nagappan 's style is easy and fluid. There is no trace of self-consciousness as she takes a reader along on a gentle, not-too-bumpy coming of age ride, from the time she discovers the power of teenage crushes, to her realisation that a first kiss does not necessarily lead to a permanent relationship. Exploring familiar teenage themes of friendship, ambition and competition, Isha also discovers the slightly dark side of betrayal and disillusionment. Her characters are credibly created and the situations she deals with are pretty universal. For any young person dealing with today's complex emotional terrain and negotiating a host of inter-personal challenges, Isha's slim book provides a morality tale that examines right from wrong, without being preachy or pedantic...."

Shobhaa de

Mumbai, March 2016

Chapter 1

I was packing all the things that I needed, before leaving for Pune. Choosing just a few things to take with me seemed so difficult, no wonder I pushed doing this packing to the last minute. As I looked around my room, all I could see were memories. Things that were so insignificant to me just two days ago were seen in a new light now. Every single thing seemed to be way too important for me to leave behind now. In case you are wondering why I am being overly sentimental about my room, it is because I am leaving for college in Pune, in less than two days and I just decided to finish my final packing. Apart from the necessities such as clothes and toiletries, I had so much more that I wanted to take with me. During this quest for finding things to take with me, I found my memory box. I have had this with me from the age of nine. Memories in the form of diaries, tickets, photos, pebbles, shells, crushed paper, letters, dried flowers, keychains, old doll shoes, my dog's old collar tag, wrist bands, ID cards, name tags, and so much more are kept in this box. I still remember the reason as to why I started filling this box with these things. Few years ago, one day my mom told me to clean my room and dispose all the unwanted things like little shells and marbles, which I tend to collect. I did not have the heart to throw away few things and so I hid them in a wooden box and kept it aside. With time, I added things that are of value to me in that box and kept filling that box with stuff that would otherwise get lost, if kept out. Whenever I feel depressed, I open that box and look at all the treasures it contains, and this makes me feel much better. Each tiny piece of "junk" in that box has a story behind it…Some happy, some sad but every single thing was just as important to me. This wooden box also held all the stories that made me who I am today. All those decisions you make in your teen years, small or big, create you. All your school day experiences actually guide you for a better life. Going to college seemed like so much fun just last week, but now it hit me that it is going to be a totally new environment. This means that I am going to leave my cozy little bubble in the comfort zone and get out into a totally new world. These things of my teen years in this box just gave me a fuzzy feeling in my heart and brought a smile to my face. What I seemed to realize now was the fact that most of these things in the box seemed to remind me of the time when I was around fifteen or sixteen years. That is when every small issue seemed like the end of the world. The time when I started realizing how people can be and about how important the five-letter word "trust" was. Those years just seemed so distant now, but thinking back, those few years made me stronger and achiever. Let me see how much of those years I actually can remember.

"At last…home sweet home, but it is kind of warm here" I said as I fell onto my bed after returning from the airport. The summer of 2012 was coming to an end as we just returned from Europe. Italy and Spain were amazing, especially when you travel with your family and friends. We created so many memories that I will cherish for the rest of my life and hopefully they will too. The weather in those countries was so pleasant and the chill winds were something I had gotten so used to over the past few days, so it took me sometime and some complaining to get over the heat in Mumbai. Our house, being locked up until we returned just made it even hotter and hence worse. It was not even two hours after reaching Mumbai that I wished to go back to Spain and Italy – especially the cruise. It was all amazing experiences, but I guess it was time for me to return from the wonderful holiday, which felt like a refresh button, and go on with life. When I inserted my Indian SIM card back in my mobile phone, I expected many messages since I was not in India on my birthday. When the mobile phone was switched on, there were so many notifications from various messaging apps and social media forums. Few notifications for my birthday and few for other things; I have also received a few calls from people I know. But Aaliya, my best friend, seemed to be the one who called me maybe several times? So without checking the time, I called her sister's mobile phone since hers was switched off, and I think they saw the caller ID because Aaliya picked up the mobile phone and started saying "What the hell Al? You didn't even pick one phone call – and my mom says I am not fit to have a phone, me! I so need to talk to you and you go off happily holidaying? What the hell?" and she was talking so fast that I did not understand anything, so I said "Whoaaa! Aaliya… Calm down. Slowly – okay?" and then, she said at a slower pace "Ron failed and he is in our class this year!" Hearing this, at first I smiled because upon returning from a holiday away from all the high school drama, this little detail about how Aaliya's ex-boyfriend failing and staying in our class just did not seem like the biggest deal to me. Then, I stopped smiling realizing once that Aaliya did not get the reaction she was expecting from me and she said "Hello?" Then I replied, "Hmm…just processing that, wait." She had just gotten over him and since the break-up was pretty bad, there was a part of her that still wanted him back…she had just started becoming normal – why did that fool have to fail?! And I said "Um... Okay...Uh... Just do not talk to him much and ignore him as much as possible" and she said "That will be a little tough when he is in my section, right?" and I said "Oh God! Not again Aaliya – you are not going to get emotional again. Are we clear? He is your past and will remain your past. And it is not like he told you he still had feelings for you..." and there was a brief silence and I asked again "Right?" and she said "Not exactly." And from behind, her sister pulled the mobile phone and said "He told her, he still wanted to be friends and that he doesn't know if he can or will like any other girl as much as he liked her so she is pretty confused about what she has to do" and then I said "Why would he go do that? She was just getting over him" and Aaliya's sister said "I know right. And Aaliya's even stupider to have to actually sit and worry about this...wait I will give it to her – oh! And...did you see any cute guys in Spain?" she asked "Not really Amara" I said laughing and she gave the mobile phone to Aaliya and I asked "WHEN did this happen?" and she said "three days after you left," "Am I the first one to know after your sister?" I asked and she replied "Yeah!" and I said "You have kept this somewhat to yourself since then?" and she replied "Yes... I wanted to know what you would say and then go tell the other girls, you know, just like that" and I said "AW...ok now see you have to try and ignore him whenever you see him because you and I both know that even though you are getting over him, you are not there yet and talking to him is just going to make things worse" and she said after thinking of many possible awkward scenarios where they both would meet and have to talk in school she finally let out a deep breath and said that this is why she needed to talk to me. And I said "We will take care of this for sure when we meet next week, okay?" and she said "okay. Did you finish your homework?" and I said "I have a book review on one book from a series, I am choosing The Hunger Games, and I also have to do that article about that Indian women having freedom or not topic… I don't know how boys will write about this though" and she said "They won't – the teachers sent all the boys mails saying that their topic is changed to 'Do violent video games have an effect on children's minds.' Ha!" and I giggled and said "Yeah, and by the way – you are coming for my cousin sister's wedding Sangeeth practice from tomorrow right?" and she said "Yeah… Gia's wedding right? Obviously – I have known her from the time I have known you!" and I just laughed – Gia is my cousin sister who is twenty-two years old. (There is an eight-year gap between the both of us, but we are really close.) "Gia is living in Bangalore now cause she got a good job there and she is getting married to guy who is coincidentally our family friend's son, they fell in love and all that cheesy cute stuff apparently (those were the exact words Gia told me) and they are getting married on the first of June and their Sangeeth (the day when the families from both sides put on a show or event with music and dancing – like an after party) is on the third of June. We exactly have nineteen days for the Sangeeth and Gia told me to bring a few of my friends for the Sangeeth practice because they need more people for the performances and kids will be nice, and I clarified to her that we are not exactly kids – we are fifteen, to which she just laughed and said that she felt like time went by very fast and that she feels like she was just changing my diapers yesterday to which my reaction was – "Ewwww!" and she just laughed. So I called a bunch of my close friends like Naina Aaliya, Sam, Jai, and Raj.

Raj was coming anyway because he is my cousin as well and Jai was a family friend so he was also coming too. It was going to be so much fun! I talked to Aaliya for another twenty minutes on the mobile phone and then told her to be at my place the next day by 1 pm because the Sangeeth practice was at Gia's house (her parents live in Mumbai so the house was not sold after she left to Bangalore). But the practice started only at 4 pm. Other people already met two days ago and discussed about what to do, so all we had to do was go there and learn the moves, have fun, and make props.

Chapter 2

The next day, Aaliya and Naina came home early and I showed them what I bought from the holiday trip, and we were talking about the Ron and other stuff and we had little lunch and left at 3:30 pm to Gia's house. The guys said that they would come there when their parents come there. Raj was a part of the bride's side obviously and Jai was from the groom's side because he was very close to them and in some freaky way related to them too. As we reached, three of Gia's school friends came to me and hugged me so tight that I felt like puking. Later, Gia saw me from across the room and her charming smile stretched from one ear to the other. She came and hugged me, and for some reason, we both started laughing and behind her was Sid, her fiancé. He said "Hey Al!" and I said "Hey Sid! I mean, should I call him 'Bhiya' or something?" And Sid said "Please, I have known you for almost ten years, you've never called me that before so don't start now – it'll make me feel old you know?" and Gia just said "Yeah yeah! And we wouldn't want that, would we?" and I just laughed and we all went upstairs and Gia started talking to Naina and Aaliya too. When we went up, I was shocked to see Jai, Sam, and Raj there earlier than us. At first, I did not know how I would dance before them but slowly I started getting over that since the guys were pretty terrible themselves. Gia had an idea of doing this Sangeeth like a small musical – their story in the form of a dance/drama. We all struggled a little for the steps too, but at the end of the day we all got it. I had a lot of fun, especially when we had breaks and the others had to dance, because at that time we got to see them and laugh at few of the guys cheesy moves. The next day Naina called and said that she could not come for the practice because she had to go to her hometown to see her grandparents and she said that she was sorry because she did not know till now and that is why she was informing me so late. So it was just Aaliya and I now. We went for rehearsals and had lot of fun. Whenever we got the time, Aaliya and I would talk about school and Ron and she would start teasing me at times with people but somehow we would change the subject. Soon our moves got better as we all learned our steps and cues properly and got more organized, but Gia being the perfectionist got tensed at times when things did not go too well. Once when we had a break, Jai pulled me aside and I said "Whoa! What happened?" and he said "Sorry, I just had to tell you something…" and I said "Yes…" and he said "Ron might have failed and he might be in Aaliya's section" and I gave him this look which meant "I KNOW" and I think he understood because he said "Wait…you knew that?" and I said "Yes! Aaliya told me everything. Who told you?" and he said "Uh…. No one" and I said "Yeah right, you just magically know it… C'mon, you can tell me" and he said "You cannot tell Aaliya" and I said "okay, I won't" and he said "When we went to school to collect the report cards I got to know, because Ron told me that there's a possibility… and I think he's kidding but maybe he's telling the truth… and I didn't want to tell Aaliya this because I told Ron that I won't tell anyone." I said "Well, You told me…" and he said "Yeah but…uh…you already knew and this is different" and I said "okay…but anyway Aaliya knows… Ron told her himself" and Jai said "Oh… Ron did?" and I said "I think so…I mean she didn't tell me who told her but who else knows about this?" and he said "well…about that… Sam knows because I told him about it" and I said "oh well that explains everything…he must have told her obviously…. He must have also told her that Ron said that he is over Aaliya but isn't ready for any other relationship yet" and Jai said "Yeah…Ron said that he was over her but isn't ready for a relationship YET…he never said that he will NEVER be able to be in a relationship…make that clear to Aaliya" and I just nodded and all the worries about Ron joining us next year just vanished a little since now I know that it is just a little possibility. And he never said that he was not ready for a relationship, he just was not ready for it YET. And since we were standing partially outside the room and I could hear Sid say "back to practice, spread out guys… 5, 6, 7…" And we went in and joined the group and that too right on time because we reached our correct positions when Sid said one. And while we were dancing Aaliya smiled and lightly whispered "What did he tell you outside?" and I said "Nothing." And she said "Oh! So you guys weren't talking about anything outside – just stood there for five minutes doing nothing?" and I smiled and said "I will tell you later." I thought I could tell her something else because she would not like it if she knows that Ron is still talking about this to everyone and how he is tensed in being in her class and about how he was feeling about it to her friends. I did not want to keep talking to her about him since I was supposed to help her get over him. After the dance was over Gia literally jumped up and clapped and said "Yay! At last!" and all of us started clapping for ourselves too. Our whole dance drama was like a mini cheesy film. There was a song for the introduction of the groom where he is portrayed as the guy that every girl wants but cannot have and there is another introduction song for the bride where she is portrayed as the perfect girl who is desired by all. These two "perfect people" meet at a wedding. In real life, even though Sid and Gia knew each other for so long, it was a wedding when they actually started talking and bonding. I was there and I clearly remember how engrossed they were in each other's conversations. From then on, they hit it off and now we are here, at their wedding. Coming back to the Sangeeth, the next scene was supposed to show the whole "Falling in Love Phase": Late night phone calls, waiting to meet each other, dating, and so on. This was all shown in one song with the help of the props perfectly. After that was "The Proposal" where the groom makes the bride's friends bring her out to the place where they had their first date and she acts so shocked but was actually expecting it. And right after that, we start dancing and move out of stage and into the dance floor and bring people in from the audience, and from that point on, the DJ plays music as he desires and everyone start dancing. I thought that this whole thing was going to be amazing and right after practice we all went downstairs to eat. Raj, Sam, Jai, Aaliya, and I sat together and were eating and talking because the friends from the bride's side were talking to her about college and the bridegroom's friends were talking to him and few were just talking on their mobile phones so we sat as a group but were also talking to the others and the music was playing from the iPod speakers. It was like a camp out with friends and family just that it was indoors and there was air conditioning. I was sitting in between Aaliya and Jai. Aaliya whispered into my ears "You told me you would tell me what he told you later, tell me now" and my mind was just rushing through all the possible things to say, I could say

1. He asked me why Naina did not come today. But why would he pull me out and ask me that? He could have asked Aaliya if that was the case.
2. He told me he did not get a step. Now that is just stupid – Aaliya would detect that lie instantly.
3. He was discussing ideas with me about what to do for the group activity the English teacher told us to do. Yes that is stupid, but hey! I am caught and that might just work out.

So I turned to her and said this hoping she asks no further questions. She looked pretty disappointed and asked "He pulled you out alone to ask you this? That's all?" and I said "Yeah. Why?" and she said "Nothing." And I felt a sense of relief. Just then Jai whispered "Did she ask you anything about what happened outside?" and I said "I took care of it. I'll tell you about it later" and Sam turned to both of us and just then I stopped talking so Sam just smiled and whispered something to Jai and Jai whispered something back to him. I did not know what was going on but I really did want to know! I hate the feeling of curiosity. There's a proverb "Curiosity killed the cat," which basically means that curiosity can put you in danger. And after knowing what danger it can put me in after listening to stories and personal experiences, I still tend to be curious about the tiniest things that happen in front of me but I never know clearly.

We all went back home exhausted that day, and as soon as I reached my home, I received a call from Aaliya and she said "I just heard something from Sam and I wanted to tell you…" and I said "okay…tell me then" and she said "Sam and I both think Jai likes you… Just think about it – your families are so close and even you are very close to him" and I said "Is this about what happened today? Because if it is then I told you then and I am telling you now, we were only talking about the project." And Aaliya said "Not exactly... I mean, when Sam usually asks Jai if he likes someone or if he has a crush on someone and mentions any name Jai would say 'No way!' or 'Do you think I have a crush on her?' or 'she's my friend dude!' or if it's very weird he would go to the extent of sister-zoning her, but when Sam mentioned about you yesterday after the Sangeeth practice, Jai just said 'I don't know...Why? Do you think so?'" This somewhat surprised me because Jai and I have always just been best friends and I have not really thought of him that way but I did not want to make a big deal out of anything since I do not even know if these idiots were just exaggerating or whether this actually happened so I just said "Well...that...it doesn't mean that he likes me." and she said "Al! The guy just said that he 'Doesn't know if he likes you' that totally means he has a crush on you!" And I said "It's not like that...we are just very good friends and he must have meant something else..." and she said "okay fine...It's not like you are going to accept it so leave it, but just think – haven't you ever felt like he likes you? He helps you all the time by doing those tiny things that matter, always takes your side, does anything to turn your frown upside down? Even though he talks about somewhat the same things we talk about, the way he talks to you is different from his conversations with Sam or me or anyone else, right?" and I just said "Aaliya can we leave this? All that you just said is something that I would do for him too because we are best friends. Let's just leave this topic. I've got to go sleep – I'm very tired. Bye" and she said "Fine, Bye. See you tomorrow" and I disconnected the call. Then I fell onto my bed and was just thinking – Was

Aaliya right about what she said? Were Jai and I different with each other? I mean I am pretty close to him… And… Wait a minute…why am I thinking about this? No. Jai and I are just good friends. That's all. Now, if I just close my eyes and….

Chapter 3

BEEP BEEP BEEP!

Whoa! I did not set an alarm! It must be Rishab… His college started and he has to wake up every day at 6:30 am so that he can reach the college by 7 am and discuss some filmmaking project with his group mates. He wants to be a filmmaker later and I think he has good taste at times but when he bugs me I just do not like anything he does and right now he is bugging me by waking me up on my holidays! So I got out of bed and the beeping continued even as I walked across the hall to my brother's room and when I reached there and opened the door, he was still sleeping. He woke up when I went and turned the alarm off and I said "Thanks a lot!" to which he just smiled and said "Anytime!" I got irritated and slammed his door on my way out. I fell back onto my bed and stuffed my face in a pillow and I just looked up at the clock I had by my bedside, the time was 6:35 am and I was awake!! I did not know what to do, so I thought I could read the rest of The Hunger Games book so that I can finish my book report on it and so I ran into my bathroom and brushed my teeth, grabbed the book, and sat on my bed. I was on page 290 and I had to read 100 more pages after which I had to write a report on it, so I started – I thought that I would read fifty pages today and other fifty pages tomorrow. But when I started reading, it got so interesting that I could not put the book down. It was in the ninety-fifth page where I realized that I only had five pages to go so I could finish the book by today. So I finished it and really wanted to read the next book, but I had not bought it yet. Then, I sat and wrote my book report, which was a one hour process. By the time I was done, it was 11 am. I had a lot of time to kill so I did not know what to do, all I knew now was that I did not have breakfast and my stomach was aching a little so I went downstairs and opened the cabinet near the fridge to take out some cereal but I saw that someone finished my cereal and it could only be one person – MY BROTHER! Ugh! So I went to the fridge where I found a ton of healthy alternatives to much tastier food because my parents were health-freaks. I just took two slices of bread, spread jam and peanut butter on it, took a glass of lemonade and went up to my room where I watched TV and ate. Right then, my phone rang and when I picked it up it was Jai and he said "Hey!" and I could hear Sam talking in the background so I just rolled my eyes and said "Hey Jai…and Sam!" and Jai said in a little hushed voice to Sam "See… I told you she'll know that you're with me!" and then Sam said "Fine, fine" and then he came closer to the mobile phone and said "Hey!" and I said "What do you guys want?" and Sam said "We were just bored so we called. Sup?" and I said "nothing much – just watching TV. What are you guys doing?" and Sam said "We were just talking and having breakfast. Did Aaliya call you yesterday?" and as soon as Sam said that I could hear Jai cough or choke on something in the background and Sam started laughing so I said "What's going on there? Is someone choking?" and Sam said "Uh…No…Jai just swallowed his food too fast – that's all. Anyway did Aaliya call?" and I said "Yeah she did, Why?" and Sam said "No reason, I'm just bored and wanted to know stuff… Did she tell you something or ask you something?" and I asked "number one – you are acting super weird and number two – Since when are you interested in our conversations? I thought you hated 'girl talk'... Besides we just spoke about the Sangeeth and the wedding. That's all!" and Jai said from behind Sam "Put the phone down Sam!" but Sam just continued "Oh! She didn't tell anything else...anyway talking about the Sangeeth... What were you and Jai talking about yesterday in the practice sessions?" and I said "You seem to be very interested in my conversations with others..." and Sam said "Like I said earlier, I am just bored... So I am eager...that's all" and I said "Sam! All we spoke about was the group project in school. Jai and I are in the same group so we were discussing some ideas" and Sam said "Oh...of course you did! Anyway leave that, you know me, I am just kidding around you see?" and I said "Right. Of course you were. Anyway what did you think Aaliya told me anyway?" and then Sam said "Aah.... I just thought...." And Jai said from behind "okay Sam we have to go... " And Sam said "But" and then the phone got disconnected. I do not know what to do for Sam to stop this, I am sure Aaliya is a part of whatever he is doing too.

It is 12 pm now and I finished my book report, got ready, finished breakfast and am still bored. I just sat down on the couch in the hallway and started drawing in my sketchbook. And I decided that I was not in the mood for drawing and wanted to check if anyone were online, so I went back to my room and took my mobile phone from the shelf it was charging in. There were two messages; one message was from Jai that read "Sorry about the call. Will see you at practice."

And the second message was from some dumb mobile service. All my family friends have either school or college today so they will be busy. I felt like the only jobless person in the city! It is not because I was alone but because I did not know what I wanted to do. I like being alone at times when I have something to do or when I am tired and just want to laze around but today was the day I was alone and jobless. Not such a great combination. School did not seem so bad anymore. I continued with my drawing, but this time I just started drawing abstract patterns and put down whatever was on my mind and it actually felt nice. The music was on next to me and I realized that as the songs kept changing, the way I drew kept changing along with it. The music was having an impact on my mood and I was so engrossed in this that I lost track of time. I was then distracted by a call from my mom (Dad and mom had to go to Delhi for a meeting and so they told my aunt who lives across the street to check on me every day and my mom also told my maid to keep the doors locked 24/7 and only to open the door after looking through the peep hole. P.S she took one hour to teach my maid that!). My mom called and asked how the practice was going on and when it was today and if my aunt came and checked on me today and I said that she came once when Rishab left the house for college and then I told her that practice was good and after talking for some time mom had to go for the meeting so we disconnected the call and then I went and sat in front of the TV and luckily the movie "Miss Congeniality" was going on and even though I have watched that movie a million times, it was better than nothing. And when I was watching the movie, Sam called and he said "Hi!" and I said "Hey…" and he said "Actually, none of our cars are free today after 4 pm but the Sangeeth practice is at 5:30 pm and we didn't really want to go there early and wait so Jai's driver is going to drop us at your place at 4:00 pm and we can go to the Sangeeth together okay?" and I said "Well, Aaliya is coming here at 4:30, so okay. Yeah. You guys come here and we can go from my place." And Sam said "Great! See you soon Al." I was watching TV and texting Sam and Jai (both of them were texting through Sam's phone) and that's when I heard the bell ring, I did not know who it could be since my parents and brother were not at home, so I went downstairs and tried calling our maid but she was not there so I went and looked out through the window on the right side of the door before opening and I could not see anyone standing there, I did not understand – I was sure I heard the bell ring then… "Boo!" Aaliya jumped in front of the window, I just jumped back and sighed. Aaliya has been doing this for the past three years whenever she came home and I continued to fall for it. I opened the door and she came in and I asked her "Weren't you supposed to come at 4?" and she said "Yeah but my mom wanted the car early for her to go out and I tried calling from home but your phone was busy so I just got dropped" and I just nodded. Then she kept her bag on the sofa of the TV room and slopped down on the beanbag. I sat on the sofa next to her and we were just talking when she started "the topic." I knew she would start this – "So…. Did Sam call you again?" and I just rolled my eyes and said "Yes…why?" and she said "No reason, just that…well if you accept it or not Jai and you would make a great couple" and I said "How many times do tell that we don't like each other and that we are only good friends, maybe even best friends but nothing more than that?" and Aaliya said "You don't talk to other guys like you talk to Jai, it's just different and…" I cut in and said "Even Sam and you are best friends and you have spoken to him about things you wouldn't even tell Tina or Naina, does that mean you guys like each other and should be in a relationship?" and all Aaliya said was "But… Well…Ugh! I hate it when you make sense. And the only reason I am bringing all the small things up is because I feel like he is leaving subtle hints to show you that he likes you and you're not picking them up" and I said "Stop. I don't like Jai. And he doesn't like me either. That's all. Okay?" and she said "Fine…."

Chapter 4

Five more days for the Sangeeth and more importantly three more days for the wedding! And that means – tension, decorations, music, more relatives and friends, house being jam packed and a lot of noise – and I do not know why but gold, red, and white seem to be the only colors I see right now! My cousin is being taken to every single relative, half of whom she did not even know existed, and she is having this smile plastered on her face throughout. As all of Sid's relatives have not arrived yet, he was just sitting on the couch watching everything and grinning. I was wearing a kurthi, which was a little itchy in all the odd possible spots, and I was just talking to the few relatives I know. Just then we heard the bell ring and I thought, "now who could that be?!" And in came caterers with big containers and the ladies who put mehendi (henna) for all women in the family. Since I am Gia's first cousin I have to put mehendi for my hands and feet apparently. So I had to sit in that one place for a long time, waiting for the lady to finish doing her thing and then had to wait until it dried properly for it to leave a dark red impression once I washed it off. I do not like the smell of mehendi at all, but the whole house was filled with that aroma because, well, every lady in the house had it on their hands. Scratch that… it's not aroma. It's stench. After this was over, my parents and I left to home; my brother did not come with us because he had no idea what to do if everyone is only going to be wearing mehendi and dirtying the house. He might come for practice with me tomorrow because he is performing in the Sangeeth.

THE WEDDING IS TOMORROW!!! Oh my god! Everyone is happy, feeling tensed, excited, and overjoyed tensed? Today we had practiced almost throughout the day, and Gia and Sid were there for few parts and the other parts were a surprise for them (the part which we enacted was how they met, it is basically like a little musical). Gia and Sid went to see the wedding hall and the reception and the Sangeeth hall to make sure the flower decorations, the camera settings, and everything else was perfect. All other people were laughing and feeling happy because there is a wedding in the family after quiet sometime while others were crying because their little girl and little boy grew up and are leaving the house. A wedding house is one place where different emotions and experiences fill the atmosphere: it may be the feeling of the emotional mothers or the happiness of the little girls wearing mehendi for the first time and dancing around in their perfect little gaghras…Oh it was just like a Bollywood movie. There were even people practicing for the Sangeeth, which even made it seem like one of those synchronized dances that you view in the movies. Sam, Jai, Aaliya, and I were sitting after finishing practicing and Rishab was still dancing, and for some reason watching my brother dance was funny even though he dances pretty well. That's when few of my cousin's college friends came and were talking to me…few of them even went to school with her so they have seen me since I was a baby even. We were laughing about something that I cannot seem to remember and that is when I saw him, he was wearing a good fitting black suite and had a drink in hand. He came up to me and said "Hey Al, don't you remember me?" It is my uncle Rajesh. I remembered him clearly; he is Gia's uncle, her mom's brother. Our families used to be very close and he used to be the best uncle. He had a girlfriend who he had been with for five years and I already used to consider her my aunt from the first time I met her and when my uncle proposed she accepted and it was not really a shock to anyone. They were a happy couple and the next step was a baby. But that just could not happen as the doctors said that she had some problem so she could never give birth to a child, and after knowing this, both became very sad. My aunt would cry every day because she had always wanted the life that she had planned and a baby after two years of marriage was a part of "the plan" that was not possible because of her; seeing this, uncle Rajesh became upset, frustrated, why could not they have a baby? He tried to divert his mind by staying at work more than he used to so that he did not have to see the woman he loved so much cry. What he did not think of was to be with her through this and help her. We all used to meet every weekend before this incident but slowly they stopped coming anywhere out and we lost touch. They moved to Delhi because Rajesh uncle's boss liked his work and transferred him to the main office there. And we heard from him only one year later but even then I did not get to meet him or talk to him much. All of this happened when I was eight and now I am fifteen.... Six years have passed and I felt like a lost a great uncle, it felt like I lost him forever. I wanted to help but I was too young to even understand the whole issue when I was just eight. I was also told that I should not get into their business, but I was really ready to do anything to bring back their happiness and to bring back that uncle who would do anything for me. This man who was standing in front of me was not the uncle who was filled with sadness and pain, he was healing and it showed in his shining eyes that were smiling, I then said "Of course

I remember you" I then hugged him and he hugged me back tightly, like my dad would after coming back from a long work trip where he missed my brother and me. After that he said clearing his throat "So…where's the beautiful bride?" and I just pointed at Gia who was surrounded by a group of happy women hugging and congratulating her. Then I asked in a soft tone "Is aunty here?" and he said "Yes, she wouldn't miss Gia's wedding now would she? She's there" he pointed at aunt Astha who was talking to Gia's mom. She looked very pretty, as usual. She did not look depressed or sad; in fact, she looked much better than the person I remembered to be sitting on the staircase crying every day. I smiled and walked towards her. I tapped her shoulder and she turned around. When she saw me she gave me a big smile and hugged me…the hug was the followed by a kiss on the cheek and I swear I think I saw a tear in her eye. She then said "Look at you Al…you have become taller and you are looking so pretty…oh all you kids are growing up too fast!" and she hugged me again and I just laughed and hugged her back. Then we were talking about where they live now and how I would love their house and which grade I was in and what Rishab was doing. It felt good to talk to aunt Astha, I started remembering how she used to support me in the stupid fights I used to have with Rishab, how she used to bake me her famous cookies which I loved and she even taught me to make them. Later I went to my friends and she went to talk to others. After everyone left, only the closest relatives and few relatives who were staying in the house were present, uncle Rajesh and aunt Astha made an announcement.

"We tried a lot, we went through a lot of procedures to try to get a child, but it just isn't happening…we were so sad and frustrated that we forgot about our loved ones. We went to Delhi and never spoke to all of you. We pitied ourselves so much that we forgot the good times we've had with our family. So what if we can't have a child now? We can't do anything about it and we have eventually got to move on over that fact someday so why not today? Alisha, Gia, Rishab, and Aahan are like our own children and watching them grow is like watching our own children grow…. So from now on we are not going to stay away or drift apart, Rajesh has got transferred back to Mumbai and I got a job as a columnist in the Indian Beat Magazine too." My mom went and hugged my aunt and said "I am so happy for you" and everyone were very happy. Soon we heard small sobs followed by laughs and a whole lot of hugs. Everything is going back to normal and I felt very happy about this. But I still felt sad that they could not have a child of their own because they would make great parents and pamper their child to the fullest… I was just thinking of other ways for them to have a child and I guess I was thinking too deeply because I thought out loud by saying "adoption" in a soft tone. I guess it was pretty soft because the only people who heard it were aunt Astha, uncle Rajesh, and Gia, and instantly I said "Oh sorry, I was just thinking…I don't know why I said it out loud…sorry" and aunt Astha just smiled and said "It's okay sweetie, you are right. We thought of Adopting a child but we really need to love the child like our own and no one from the family should have anything against him or her and well there are other issues too….so it might not be the best option" and I just nodded and smiled.

The wedding just got over and now my legs are aching because of me running from one place to the other for taking flowers, water for the bride, people to seats, talking to people, and doing the rituals I am supposed to do as part of the family. Apart from this, the gaghra and jewelry I was wearing made this even more uncomfortable. After the wedding was over, we all went to the hotel rooms we have booked to freshen up so we can get ready for the evening reception planned to take place there. We all reached garden area of the hotel by 5 pm for the reception, while other people began to arrive there from 5:30 pm. The garden was beautiful with pretty shiny golden serial lights on the trees and few yellow- and red-netted lanterns hanging from few trees. The buffet tables were arranged and there was a small stage with a sofa that was very pretty and there were flower decorations behind it. There were many round tables with seating around it with one small lantern on each table. The evening was so beautiful and then came Gia. She looked stunning like a princess wearing a red sari. Her makeup and hair were perfect. I always thought Gia and Sid made a cute couple and they continued to prove me right by sitting in the couch teasing each other and acting like five year olds. The DJ in the side played some soft romantic songs to "set the mood." After sometime, everyone started arriving, dressed at their best with different sized gifts. Few came with the gifts wrapped with the wrapper of the shop they got it from, so few of the brands I saw were Burberry, Lladró, and Swarovski. I was then distracted by my cousin Aahan; he snuck up behind me and said "Hi." And I did not even have to turn to see who it was because I can recognize that deep irritating voice anywhere. "Hey Aahan," I said. Aahan was Gia's younger brother, he is in eleventh grade now and he has a band of his own. They have not done any gigs, but the band was formed only a month ago and they are planning to go for "The Ultimate Band Hunt" contest. They are still searching for a few more singers for back-up and duets. Aahan plays lead guitar and his three friends play keyboard, drums, and guitar, respectively. All of them sing each verse, I have seen them practice once and they were pretty good. They do not write songs yet, they only make covers for/of other artist's songs. I sang with them once too, and it was fun. Aahan and I were talking when Rishab came and told us that we had to help with something. So after that, the whole evening was only helping with small things and talking to guests and later talking to Raj and Jai.

The next day was just so hectic! Few people could not come for practice on the day of the Sangeeth before the main event started so we had to compensate practice accordingly and Gia wants everything to be perfect, while all Sid cares about was whether everyone are having a good time. Ah! that is why they make a good pair – they balance each other. Anyway, now coming back to the point, my legs are going to break and fall apart, instead of going to the Sangeeth I will have to go to the hospital. But Gia is too tensed to notice. She has always been such a perfectionist, which is a good thing, but we really need a break to just catch a breath maybe. But we all just continued dancing because no one wants to upset Gia, or else we will have to face some severe consequences. At last, practice was over and we all left home except for the people staying in the house. I went home, fell on my bed, and the next thing I remember was I fell fast asleep. Next day, I woke up at 8 am and my mom came into my room with the clothes I need to wear for the Sangeeth. I then took the clothes to change into before the Sangeeth along with my makeup and jewelry and left to Gia's house. Practice was only at 2 pm but I just left. I reached there and Gia, Sid, Aahan, and Meera (Gia's best friend from college) were in the TV room watching a movie. When I went in, Gia smiled and I sat down next to her on the sofa. She seemed pretty calm even though the Sangeeth was that evening. Then she said, as though she read my mind "I have decided not to get tensed anymore because I know it's of no use....you guys WILL do well" and I do not know if she was really saying that or if she is subtly trying to say that she expects it to be good, because Gia has this weird way of "leaving hints," she thinks she does it subtly but actually she does it in such a way people do not even realize that it could possibly be a hint. But since we have been with her for quite some time we understand her stupid hints....sometimes. She was still looking at me so I just nodded and gave a thumbs up and when I turned around I could see Aahan giving me this confused look and he mouthed "Was that a hint that she wants the thing to be good?" and I just shrugged. After the movie was over, Gia and Sid had a quick breakfast and went to check if the people have started setting the banquet in which the Sangeeth was going to take place, and Aahan and I were just talking at home and slowly by 1 pm everyone started arriving for practice. As soon as everyone came, we all started our final practice because as Gia said: we WILL have to do well.

The Sangeeth was amazing!!!! I got ready at Gia's house. I changed into my gaghra, wore the jewelry, set my hair properly and ran down. Everyone was there except for Gia who came five minutes after me. She looked stunning! She usually looks really pretty too, but today she looked prettier in her beautiful deep pink saree. We all left for the hotel and the banquet was amazing! There was a dance floor next to the small stage and there were chairs all around the dance floor and behind the seats was a long bar table behind which, obviously, were bartenders. What I liked the most was the lighting: it was a little dim and pretty. After the performances started, we had a lot of fun dancing and Gia and Sid loved that little skit. After that, the dance floor's bright white lighting was on and the other lights went even dimmer and the DJ started playing mainstream Hindi and English songs that brought almost everyone onto the dance floor. Jai, Aaliya, Raj, and I went for dinner only at 12:30 am. After we finished eating, Jai called me outside and I thought that he was leaving so I accompanied him outside the banquet and towards the exit and that is when he said "Has Aaliya been talking to you about…us?" and I just said "What?" and he said "Al…. I really like you…more than you think" and I do not know if it was because I was a little sleepy or just because I am stupid but I laughed. I felt so stupid after that when I found out that he was actually serious and I said "Wait…as a friend right?" and he said "No….more than a friend… I thought you already knew that…" and I said "No Jai! I didn't, I just thought that Aaliya and Sam were kidding around. I'm so sorry… I do love you but just as a friend. Nothing more than that" Jai was quiet for some time and then I said "Please tell me that this will not affect our friendship" and he said "Yeah don't worry it won't. Now I've got to go so I'll see you later, bye!" and saying that he walked to his car and drove away. I was left standing there knowing that even though he said that this will not affect our friendship, it will.

Chapter 5

Although there were some people still there in the reception, I left by 1 am, so I do not really know what happened after that. Rishab stayed back and said that his friend could drop him and I guess he had fun because he came back home only at 3 am.

The next day I woke up, went downstairs and made myself a peanut butter sandwich, took a glass of milk, and sat with my parents at the table. Later my brother walked down the stairs looking as sleepy as ever. Seeing his state, my mom told him to go back upstairs and sleep because if he goes to college like this then they might send him back or literally throw him out of class. I am guessing he was completely ok with that idea because he just gave a dopey smile and walked back upstairs. I took a bath and said bye to my mom who was going for work and sat in front of the computer to finish my holiday assignments. I had something due in almost every subject, but I had finished most of it before I left for Spain. I just had to now finish the rest. It was fourth of June today and my school reopens on the sixth of June. Two more days!! Then school starts, new students, new books...correction – new BIG, FAT books, tougher studies. Plus since its tenth grade, we will have the Public Board Examinations at the end of the year. Basically I am going to do nothing but study for this entire year. Our seniors who just completed their exams have scared us enough by telling us that we will forget what sleep will be and fun was out of the question...we used to tease them then and now I guess it was our turn.

I could not concentrate much with all the stuff that happened with Jai. He was my best friend and I do not want to lose him just because of this. Why does this stuff have to be this tough? Why could not this be like one of those things you just forget and move on? I know that I am being stupid and impractical but still....why?

June sixth!!! I am getting ready for school now; just put on a half sleeve blue shirt with skinny jeans, combed my hair and tied it up in a ponytail, wore black sneakers, wore my ID card, took my school bag, and ran to the car. Jai texted me last night asking me to leave that "incident" and told me that I was right and that this should not affect our friendship. I know that he would try to be as normal as possible, but there will be something missing in him. People say that time heals everything; maybe it will take us back to what we were? I was running late and if I reached school late on the first day then I am doomed! I kissed my mom and dad on the cheek and said bye as I was running down the stairs. I ran into the car and told my driver to drive as fast as he could. Thank God I reached there on time, actually a little early even – that was very surprising and then I realized that my watch was ten minutes fast.... better than being late though. I went to my class and looked around; Jai, Tina, Sam, Naina, and few other people were there in the class. I went to them and Sam said "Not bad! I thought you would either be here thirty minutes late today or that you would be running and panting and your hair would look like a raccoon's nest because you would have thought that you were late, but you look fine and you are ten minutes early! I'm impressed" and I just gave a sarcastic laugh and said "Is that supposed to be a joke?" and Sam just stuck his tongue out. Then Tina pulled me aside and I said "Hey! How was your trip?" and she said "Good, I had fun. And guess what?"

and I said sarcastically "What? You love someone?" and she just kept quiet and smiled, I widened my eyes "Shut up! You love someone? When did this happen?" and she said "Not love someone! You know Aryan right?" and I said "Aryan? From tenth grade? The guy who you make fun of each time I talk about?" and she said "Yeah… I mean he's my neighbor right? So I spoke to him once or twice and we texted and all and he was so sweet and I don't Love him, I just like him. He doesn't even know it yet. I'm sure he doesn't like me anymore than a friend but what's the harm, huh?" and I just smiled and nodded. What's the harm? Well, I know… Just before summer she could not stand Aryan and now she likes him? And she has only spoken to him like thrice! And Aryan did not tell me anything about this….I need to go talk to him and Tina is usually very practical, how did this even happen? And what if they go out? Oh my god! Wait… This is not anything related to me and I am not in a relationship with him…so why do I care? Well I just want to know since I'm his friend…But it will be really weird if Tina and Aryan go out for some reason. Not that I don't want them to go out, it's just that when it comes to relationships Tina has this weird knack of jumping into it so soon and hurting herself in the bargain. While I was thinking all of this, Naina and Aaliya came… Aaliya said "Al and I are in one class but Tina in section 'B' and Naina is in section 'C'…And the most important thing is that Ron didn't fail! But he shifted schools… He moved to some other school because they are offering him a sports scholarship and later would help him find the right college for him to pursue athletics as a career" and I was so relieved to hear this…then Naina and Tina were talking about that to Aaliya when I said "I will be right back…two minutes" and I went upstairs to the tenth grade block. Meera and Aryan were standing outside their class and talking when they saw me and Aryan said "Hey! If it isn't Alice" and I said "How come you never told me about Tina?" and Meera said "Oh! Tina? When did that happen?" and Aryan gave me this confused look "What about her?" and I said "Before you used to hate her because she always teased you and stuff, now you guys have become close friends?" and he said "We are friends.... Not close and all" then Meera went into her class and Aryan said in a hushed tone "Why? Did she say she likes me?" and I said "Why do you care? Do you like her?" and he said "No, because few guys staying in her apartment told me that she told them that she likes me a little... But I don't like her like that at all!" and I said "Oh...ok...but don't tell her I spoke to you about this...ok? I just don't want you to get her hopes up... and since it sounds like you are flirting when you talk normally to anyone maybe she got confused" and I laughed and he said "I do not!" and I said "Do too! Now I've got to go...ok? Talk to you at break.... Bye" and he just said okay and waved and I went back down. Just in time for the final bell and Aaliya pulled me and we ran into class. We sat in the seats in the third row when a tall thin lady wearing a pretty pastel saree and color-coordinated nail polish on her neatly shaped long nails came into the class and said "Good morning class.... I am Preeti and I am new to this school. I will be your class teacher for this following year as well as your English teacher. I will give everyone their seating arrangements later" and then with her soft voice and good accent she gave us our roll numbers and assigned our houses/teams. We have four teams in our school: Ruby, Emerald, Topaz, and Sapphire and these groups have to compete amongst each other in sports, arts, academics, and other activities. This year I am in Ruby, along with Aaliya and Raj. Sam and Jai are in Emerald, Naina and Rohan are in

Sapphire, and Tina is in Topaz. I felt sorry for Tina because she is in a separate class with not many people she is close to because Tina is close only to very few people because she can be a little too judgmental, she is not really a very sweet person so to few people she can be pretty mean and that is where I can never relate to her. She is also alone in a team, but in that team she knows many juniors and few seniors so she is fine with it. Later the new students slowly went to the front and were introducing themselves. There were five new people in our section. First, a girl named Gia went up and as soon as she said her name Aaliya and I looked at each other and just laughed a little because the girl introducing herself was kind of the opposite of the Gia we know. This girl had short silky hair and she looked so innocent and she was wearing a normal pink frilly shirt and blue jeans and when she talks it is more like whispering. My cousin is almost the complete opposite, she would never wear anything pink and frilly; she has long, dark and wavy hair; when she talks its loud enough for almost the whole city to hear her and she is in no way innocent or shy. Later a girl named Kayla introduced herself, she was from Delhi, she was pretty and she wore jean shorts and a green and blue T-shirt and she had her wavy hair tied in a small plait and she wore gray sneakers. I swear I heard someone say "she's pretty hot" and someone else say "Just shut up already!" behind me so I just turned around and saw the people I expected to see – Raj and Jai. Raj did not realize I was looking and told Jai "She is…" and then he looked at me and said "Oh…Hey Al… I was just saying…" and I just rolled my eyes and turned back and looked at the front. Raj thinks pretty much half the girls look pretty and tries to flirt all the time but no one would understand that he is flirting except for himself. The third person was a guy named Akarsh; he was tall, had sun-kissed skin and had deep black eyes and dimples too. Oh and he was one of those guys that did not have to flex for you to notice their biceps…he just had to scratch his head for you to say what Aaliya said… "Ooh… He's pretty darn hot" He was wearing torn jeans and a black and blue-striped shirt and for some reason he looked vaguely familiar. He went up and introduced himself and said that he moved into a new house and since his old school was far away from there he has come to this school. Then two other guys came and spoke and apparently they from the same school and were very close. Then they were asked to go be seated and the two guys went and sat in the corner of the class and started talking as the teacher went out of the class. Kayla and Gia sat behind Aaliya and me, Kayla sat next to Jai and Gia sat shyly next to her. I turned around and saw Raj and said "Better luck next time" and he just gave me a sarcastic smile. Jai just laughed and asked if he wanted to shift places but Raj said it was ok. I turned to the two new girls and said "Kayla and Gia…right?" and Kayla just smiled and said "Yeah" and Gia looked down and nodded. I said "Welcome to K.V.R… I'm Alisha" and Aaliya turned and said "And I'm Aaliya" and I pointed at Raj and said "That's Raj…" and pointed at Jai and said "And this is Jai" and we were all just talking when someone sat in the seat beside me and said "And I'm Akarsh" I turned to him and said "We know…You just introduced yourself in front of the whole class… remember?….I'm Alisha" and he just smiled and said "Hi" Aaliya cleared her throat loud enough for me to hear and I said "Oh…and this is Aaliya" and he said "Hey Aaliya… My younger sister and you share the same name" and I said turning to Gia "And my cousin sister's name is Gia!" and she just looked at me and smiled. Later a teacher came in and called Aaliya and Jai out to talk about a sports event that was coming up in school and Raj started talking to Kayla. Gia was busy scribbling something in a small, blue notebook. Sensing the awkward silence Akarsh and I said "So…" at the same time and I just laughed. And I said "Continue…" and he said "So… When did you join this school?" and I said "fifth grade" and he said "Oh…ok" and gave his award-winning smile once again and I said "Which school are you from?" "Ivy International" he said. I widened my eyes and said "You are from Ivy?" and he said "Yeah…why?" and I said "I was in Ivy before I joined this school" and he said "Yeah… I know" and I said "You do?" and he said "Yeah… I moved from Bangalore when I was in fourth grade and we weren't in the same class but I've seen you many times in the plays and music recitals and stuff…but back then I was pretty shy so it's not a shocker that you don't remember me" and I said "No… When you were introducing yourself I thought you looked familiar" and he said "Yeah. And I was pretty short then but later I fell in love with basketball and this is the result… All I know about you was that you used to love acting and singing" and I said "Yeah… I still LOVE dramatics. I was the lead in last year's school play" and then we spoke about how he loves basketball and about the Alice in Wonderland play and the people I am still in touch with from Ivy and soon the bell rang and the class teacher came back in and started our first English class of the year.

Chapter 6

"You have all heard the saying 'to be or not to be" – That is the..." RINGGGG the break bell rang and half the boys bolted out of class not caring about the English teacher who was trying to explain a Shakespeare quote and she completed her sentence after the herd of boys ran out, then the teacher continued "... question!' Ok class, I will meet you all tomorrow. And I would want all of you to bring your workbooks tomorrow and whoever does not bring it would have to stand out of class and write "I will never forget to bring my book 100 times. And no one should inform those hooligans that ran out right now." And after she left I was surprised to see Raj and Jai still in the class, I thought they bolted out along with the rest of the boys to go play football but they were still in class. Why would they still be in class? They never do... Hmm...And Akarsh then distracted my thoughts by standing up in front of me and I said "Oh...hey, so are you going to go to the canteen or are you going to go play football with the other boys?" and he said "Well if I knew where the canteen was I would go there but I don't know where anything is except for this class....so..." and I just smiled and said "Do you want me to show you around the school?" and he said "Yes please" and I said "Two minutes...I will just be back" and Aaliya came towards me and said "Akarsh and you seem to be getting along well" and I told her about how both of us were from the same school and about how I insisted in showing him the school but how I first wanted to know why Jai and Raj and Sam were not playing football as usual. So Aaliya and I went up to them and I asked Sam "How come you guys aren't playing football today?" and he said "Hmm…we just wanted to stay back and talk about stuff" and I said raising my eyebrows "What Stuff?" and Jai said rolling his eyes "Some stupid stuff" and Raj said in an offended tone "Not stupid!" and Aaliya said "What is the STUFF?!" and Raj just stared into space. Wait a minute, he was not staring into space! He was staring at something, or should I say SOMEONE. I turned to where he was looking and found Kayla talking to Gia and I turned to Raj and said "Snap out of it already!" and I told Aaliya "Kayla stuff" and we rolled our eyes in unison. Then Sam said "just like how both of you talk about…. what's his face? Hmm….yeah! Akarsh!" and I said "We don't stare at him like Raj or try to flirt with him like you guys. Poor girl, it's her first day in this school… Let her see the good parts of it before she gets hit on by you guys" and Jai said "Hey! Not about Kayla!! We were talking about something else….Boys stuff…Raj is the only one staring at her" and Sam said "Yeah…we were talking about other stuff" and Aaliya said "okay… Now I've got to go meet Meera and tell her about the sports meet… Al you want to come?" and I said "No it's okay… I've anyway got to show Akarsh around school" and Sam opened his mouth to tease me but I just said "Sam…just keep your thoughts to yourself…ok? Now bye…see you guys later" Aaliya ran to the tenth grade corridor and Akarsh was standing outside class. Both of us walked towards the canteen… I was pointing at parts of the school and telling him what was what and randomly out of nowhere he said "I know this is pretty random but have you ever been in a relationship?" and I said "No…." and he said "So no one has asked you out?" and I said "People have asked me out but few of them I didn't even know…and others were my close friends…what about you?" and he said "Well….um…" and I said "It's okay if you don't want to tell me…" and he said "No No… Well I have only gone out with one girl and that was last year in Ivy" and I said "Well do I know her?" and he said "Maybe, It is Reena…" and I said "Reena? As in the girl who always used to show off and only had two friends who were like people who worshipped her? And this was in fourth grade. God knows how she is now" and he said "Yeah. Well she's still the same, that's why I was pretty embarrassed to tell you that. She became popular and all and even though many girls didn't like her, tons of boys liked her and at that time I liked her too…and she came and told me she liked me so we went out for like a month but then after that I couldn't even talk to her normally anymore – she was too snobby and selfish and I don't know, I just couldn't relate to her. So I broke up with her and then she started ignoring me and the fact that we ever went out" and I said "Wow… hmm…sorry to hear that" and he said "Don't be! I was so happy the instant we broke up" and while we were talking Aryan came behind me and said "Hey" and I just turned and smiled and said "Hey" and just then Akarsh said "I've got to get a few books from the office room, I will see you in class?" and I said "Yeah sure…" and then I turned to Aryan who was with Meera as always – They were best friends and since Aaliya went to talk to Meera she was there too. Just then Aryan asked me "Who's that guy?" and I said "Akarsh… New student" and Aaliya said "But he was in Ivy before coming to K.V.R and Al used to be in Ivy before she came here so he talks to her the most" and Meera said "Are you sure that's the reason he talks to her the most? Or is it something else?" and she winked at me and I said "God no. It's only because he doesn't know anyone else, but he is talking to others too" and she just laughed and nodded. Aryan then said "I swear there is nothing between Tina and me…okay?" and I said "I never said there was something!" and he said "I'm just telling you…and if she tells you something then tell her I'm not interested" and I said "No way! If she tells you that she likes you then you talk it out with her…why should I be a part of all of this?" and Aaliya said "I was just going to ask Aryan the same question… Tina came and told me to ask Aryan whether he likes her or not…so Aryan… Do you like Tina?" and he said "Didn't you hear a word I just said? No I don't…and I will tell her that myself" And then he just went back to class with his friends. And later after the break, Tina came into my class and I was with Aaliya and Jai just then and she told me "Are you happy now?" and then I said "What did I do?" and she said "Aaliya went and asked Aryan if he likes me and he told her that he would talk to me about it – he came to me and I told him I kind of liked him and he told me that he liked someone else…and at first he didn't tell me who it was but later he told me" and then I said "okay…now HOW am I to be blamed here?" and Tina said "Like you don't know…" and I said "I do not know what you're talking about" and she said "He likes you Al!" and I was just standing there in shock when Tina said that. And I said "What?! That's impossible…" and Tina said "Well to him it isn't…he told me that he really liked you and that he only thought of me as a friend and nothing more" and I said "Wait a minute…he doesn't like me and I'm sure of that…and even if he did… How can you blame me for this?" and she said "I can cause he also told me that you liked him. Apparently you told him that you liked him over the holidays. Al you could've told me that this morning. I wouldn't have embarrassed myself like this if you did" and then she stormed out of class and I was just standing there confused. Aaliya came to me and said "What was that?" and I looked at her and said "You think I know?" and then Jai said "I knew Aryan had a crush on you…" and Sam said "Wait. Al, do you like Aryan?" and I said "No." Aaliya then said "She's just upset…she says stupid things when she's upset. You know that Al, it will all be normal by tomorrow" and I said "Yeah, but how in the world am I responsible? I am not apologizing, okay? If you think I am then you are wrong because I'm not" and she said "No one asked you to apologize… Just forget about this" and I said "Who asked Aryan to do all this nonsense? Ugh!" and I just went and sat in my place and everyone else came back and the teacher came in and started teaching but all I could think of was why Aryan would even think of pulling me into his stupid issues… After that class we had games so all of us went down and we were playing basketball. After games, the last period of the day was computer Ssience. And we had to cross the tenth grade corridor to reach the class. So all of us went to class, drank water, took our computer science textbooks, and went to class. The class was locked so someone went to call the teacher while the others waited outside. Class just got over for 10 A and B so half of them were out and the rest were making noise in class. Aryan came behind me and said "Hey" and I was so upset because of what he told Tina because she did not talk to me from then and ignored me completely. I did not turn around as I always do and continued talking to Aaliya who tried giving signals to Aryan to say that I was upset and I am guessing he understood whatever she was trying to do because he came in front of me and said "What happened?" and I said "Oh well, I don't know…You just pulled me into this whole issue between Tina and you, That's all!" and he said "Oh! Hey I didn't know she would be upset with you…" and I said

"Why would you even tell her that in the first place? Why me?" and then he said "Let me explain…" and just then the teacher came and opened the door so I said "I have got to go now, just tell Tina you were kidding…please" and he said "I can't….wait…" and Aaliya said "We've got to go… C'mon" and she pulled me and we went inside the class.

We finished the computer class and I went down to class to grab my bag. Later Aaliya, Naina, and I walked down, Tina was already there next to the canteen with a new girl. Tina looked up at me and then turned and looked at Aaliya and said "Hi…." Just then Aryan walked by and pulled me by my hand away from a small crowd in the canteen, and this was right when Tina was looking at me. What perfect timing?! And I said "what?" and he said "Just listen… Tina came to me today and she told me that she liked me but when I told her that I didn't like her she started asking so many questions about why I didn't like her and you know I become fidgety when people ask too many questions, so I just said that I liked someone else and she instantly asked who and I told I liked you because she knows that Meera and I are just best friends and would NEVER be anything more and she also knew that I am the closest to you in ninth so I just said that out loud without thinking it through…. Sorry!" and I said "…well she is now really upset and she saw you pull me here too…" and he said "Do you want me to talk to her?" and I said "No…she will think that I was forcing you to do that or something and she would be ok in front of you and ignore me more…" and then he said "Oh…right…and is it such a bad thing even if I liked you? You were so pissed off?" and I said "Not that! I was pissed off because she was accusing me of doing something…but wait a minute…what do you mean even if you do like me?" and he said "No… I was just saying that even if I do…not that I do now…but if I ever do…would it be so bad?" and I just laughed and said "Calm down….If you do…not that you do now…but if you ever do…" and he said "If I ever do?" and I said "We will look into it then…now I've got to go…bye" and he just waved and I went towards Tina and Aaliya and Tina looked at me and said "Did he tell you?" and I asked "What?" and she said "Did he ask you out?" and I said "No…I went and asked him why he told you that and he said that he panicked when you asked him questions and just said that he likes someone and when you asked him who it was he said it was me because he knew you would no he was lying if he said Meera or someone else in ninth" and Tina just gave a sarcastic laugh and said "Yeah right… You know you can stop lying now?" and I said "I'm not lying! What the hell should I do to prove it?" and she said "Just leave me alone!" and I just walked away…seeing me upset and storming away Aaliya came behind me and said "Al… wait…you know she acts like this when she's upset!" and I said "You mean she accuses people and acts like that when she's upset? Oh I didn't really know that…. She has no right ok? Just because a guy doesn't like her she can't create such a big thing out of it! And anyway…she started liking this guy like one day ago?" and Aaliya said "Just give it some time… and why don't you be the bigger person and apologize?" and I just gave Aaliya this confused expression. Why should I apologize? It is not like I stole the love of her life! She stated liking him just for like the past few days and he did not like her and panicked and said that he liked me and now suddenly I am the reason they are not in a relationship? And she does not trust me even though she knows me longer than she even knew him and she treats me like shit and I am the one who is supposed to apologize? I then told Aaliya "I didn't do anything! And this is a small issue which she is making much bigger than it's supposed to be. Why should I be the bigger person? I am not apologizing for something I didn't do!" and Aaliya said "okay…that's fair…let's just see what happens…" and I said "I've got to go now…bye" and I left home. When I reached home I changed and left for music class. I put my mobile phone on silent when I was in class and left it on the table where we all keep our phones. After class, I took it and saw what I expected to see – Many messages from Jai, Sam, Raj, and Naina. Aaliya must have gone and told them what happened. There was a message from an unknown number saying "Hi." And there was a call from Jai. So I called Jai after leaving class, when I was in the car. I told him about what happened and how Aaliya asked me to apologize and how I was not going to and he said "Yeah… I don't think you should apologize…and someone needs to tell Tina to calm down" Jai always thought that Tina was someone who can be fun when she is normal but when she is upset she is irritating and talks behind people's backs so Sam and Jai were not very close to Tina because of that reason. Later I saw Sam's text asking about what exactly happened between Tina and me because there were many "versions" of the stories. And I explained the whole thing to him in one long text message and all he replies with is "oh!" I hate it when people do that. So then later Naina asked me what happened and I just copied the message I sent Sam and sent that to Naina but unlike Sam she started saying 'Oh…it's alright. You don't have to apologize but just don't get too upset and make the issue bigger' and we were texting for some time.

Chapter 7

I reached home and went to my room and jumped into my bed. After finding the most awkward looking yet comfortable position to lie down in, I texted the unknown number and this is how the conversation was:

Me: Hey… Who is this?

Unknown: A person you know…

Me: Hmm… Okay…

Unknown: A person who has dated a jerk

Me: Oh… Now that just narrows it down to…Many people I know.

Seriously…who is this?

Unknown: LOL… A new friend?

Me: Akarsh?

Unknown: And that's the right answer

After that we texted and he asked me about what happened with Tina and I copied and sent him the same message I sent Sam and Naina and he had a few questions like "Who is Aryan?" or "Is Tina always like this?" and he tried to get my mind off the topic and divert me, but it did not work. I really did not know what to do with Tina anymore. This was not the first time this was happening. Last year Tina had a problem with Jai because sometimes Jai could go overboard by making fun of people a little too much and Tina is very short tempered so that was the perfect combination for trouble. Although Jai was only kidding around, Tina took it seriously, it was a small issue – so people would actually think it is pretty silly of Tina to even think about it and waste her time, But Tina thought differently. She did not talk to Jai for a whole week and expected him to apologize for some stupid joke, but Jai could not care less. Slowly, she stopped coming out when we would all meet at a coffee shop or for a movie if Jai came. Coming to think of it she was and still is a complete drama queen. She was like one of those dramatic Hindi serial actresses who do not understand that they overdo their acting at times and that those times they make a complete fool of themselves. And that time when Aaliya, Naina, Tina, and I were talking, she started talking about how stupid Jai was and how she never really even thought of him as a friend and stuff and I just objected a little by saying "But you guys used to be pretty close…why change everything just cause of this small issue?" and that was it. She was upset with me saying that I was taking his side because I liked him. I just ignored whatever she said because I was above all that. I would not stoop that low just to prove that I do not like him any more than a friend. So I left the issue and later Jai just said sorry for namesake so that the stupid issue would be over and she tells people that I apologized too and that is why we are friends but I do not remember that part of the story at all. I just finished my homework and sat and watched TV and was texting Naina and Akarsh. Akarsh was trying to crack jokes and liven me up but how much ever I told him I was fine even though I was not he was not ready to believe me so he continued telling his weird and oddly funny "Ivy" stories and I just talked about that and laughed now and then. It actually helped in taking my mind out of the whole Tina situation. Later my parents and brother came home; we had our dinner together and I then went to sleep. But sleeping was not easy because I was a little disturbed with the whole issue. It is a small issue, but I do not like breaking relations and I knew that since Tina was not just a normal friend and she was a very close friend, if the issue does not get sorted then this would lead to other people having issues with her or me eventually and it just would not be the same anymore. But this does not mean I am going to apologize because if she was really worth it, then she would not be so hurt and she would understand that this is such a small issue and just not make it bigger. Maybe she would not? Maybe she will forget it.

I was wrong! She did not forget it and she ignored me the whole day. I am a person who would want to work stuff out, so I tried talking to her about it but she did not even listen to what I was saying and treated me like I was someone she would rather kill than be seen with so I just walked away and someone came and asked what I told her and I heard her say that I was just apologizing and that I was asking her to forgive me and that she said that she would think about it and the other girl just giggled. I do not know what was irritating her so much…I really do not. I just ignored it and walked away. After a few classes, I had to go to my locker to get something and when I opened it and I found a small note. The note read out 'Stay away from Aryan…he's mine' and obviously I knew who kept that in my locker. So I went to Tina's class. She was sitting in her place and I went to her and said "What the hell is this?" and she said "Oh… I see you got the note" and I said "I don't WANT him Tina… He's just my friend. I couldn't care less if you guys were going out. How many times do I have to say that?" and she said "I don't care about all of that…just stay away from him for some time…ok?" and I said "Why? Just because a person like you tells me not to talk to MY friend I shouldn't? You know that we are good friends" and she said "So?" and I said "Tina! Seriously… Can you hear yourself? We are just friends and normal people talk to their friends" and she said "Whatever…" and she looked back into the book she was reading and I just walked away. In class, Aaliya asked me what happened and as the teacher had come inside class I could not explain to her, instead I just passed her the note Tina put in my locker. And Aaliya just said "Just…ignore it…" and later after class Aaliya and I were talking when Tina came outside our class and called Aaliya. After she left, Sam came and said "Oh…so the issue isn't sorted yet?" and I said "No…why?" and he said "Nothing…just asking because usually you would be there with Aaliya and Tina but today…well…" and I said "I know" and then Naina came to me and said "Did you hear?" and I said "What?" and she said "Well… Tina…she kinda went and told a few people that you steal people's boyfriends and that the girls should be careful or some nonsense like that…" and I said "Since when was Aryan her boyfriend? And when did I steal him?" and Naina said "I don't know…but that's what Shruthi came and told me…but don't worry…. No one believed her because when she was talking about this Aryan kind of overheard it and told her that he was never her boyfriend and that you didn't 'Steal' him…he just didn't like Tina more than a friend…. And he told this in front of few people who spread the news. That's like the latest gossip going around – That Aryan doesn't like Tina and said no to her when she asked him out and he supported you so few people think he likes you but few other people just think he was a supportive friend. Tina was not happy when this happened" and I said "Why are everyone making this such a big issue?" and Naina said "See.... I know Tina's being super unfair and all but she started liking Aryan very soon and she liked him a lot... It was only a crush but she wasn't ready to accept that and since he wasn't saying anything to her about it she wanted to tell him, and when she told him he panicked and said that he likes you and since that came to her as a shock and she still likes him and needs a person to blame she caught onto you." I just nodded because that was exactly what happened and I knew it and that is why I thought she was very unfair and that is why I was not ready to apologize. I tried ignoring it a lot. But since Tina was a very close friend and was someone who I would share stuff with almost every day, ignoring her was actually harder than I thought it would be.

Two months have passed and along with the tougher studies and singing classes and tuitions, the issue with Tina has not become bigger. She only talks to me at times and when I feel like we are getting close again, she proves me wrong by either ignoring me or just acting like I am some pesky unwanted thing.

Somehow Tina found my Facebook ID and password and she started sending messages to Ron saying that he hurt Aaliya and that she does not want to talk to him ever again and that he should stop irritating her. I would never send him that! I know that Aaliya still has feelings for him and wants to work it out slowly or at least be friends but now he stopped talking to her and when Aaliya sent him messages asking why he was not talking he told her about how "I" told him all of this. She got upset on hearing this and asked me about this. I did not know any of this happened, and after quite some time, when I logged on to Facebook to check what Tina had sent. I did not know it was Tina who did that then, but later I saw the way she chatted with him...

it was filled with abbreviations and a lot of question and exclamatory marks.... I am close or was close to only one person who does that... Tina! But I could not jump to conclusions and no one would really believe me. But I did not know what to do? I did not want to lose my best friend over something so stupid. But that's when I thought.... Aaliya is my best friend...she knows me better than that. She would definitely understand if I explained what had happened. I tried explaining it to Aaliya but even though she wanted to believe me she really could not and now we talk but somehow I cannot help feeling that it is different and that she does not tell me everything like she used to. And this scared me.... So was it actually something that I did or was Aaliya not exactly my "best friend?" I was actually very shocked when I realized that Aaliya did not trust me anymore. Slowly Aaliya started having lunch with Tina and somehow Aaliya and I became friends who are just friends for namesake and greet each other when we meet, nothing more. Naina was with me through all of this and so was Jai. Sam totally supported me, but Sam is not the kind of guy who cannot express a lot. Usually when we start talking about this, he changes the topic. Raj did not pick sides since he was close to Tina and me and just did not talk about this like Sam and I was totally fine with it. The one who understood me the most through all of this was Akarsh. Apparently, he lives a street away from me so we cycled together and we would talk about the most random things. In few ways, he is just like me, and in few other aspects, he is my complete opposite. Sometimes when I am upset, I tend to make stupid decisions and take my anger out on something else or someone else and I feel terrible after that. I tend to feel like it is my fault even when it is not and I over think things a lot! My over thinking ruins relationships and leaves me confused, but this one bad habit that is a part of me now… I do try to control it but that is just who I am. And Akarsh is my complete opposite in that aspect, he is always so calm and if he even has to take out his anger he does that in his Karate class so he does not need to over think and ruin his peace of mind like me. Both of us are alike in the way we care for our family and friends and would do anything for them blindly. All I need is for them to trust me and I needed to trust them, and he felt the same way. We slowly started getting very close and cycling together just to talk and meet each other became a part of our day-to-day lives. One day when we were cycling, we stopped next to his apartment and we went to the terrace; on the terrace, there was a small tank and a ladder to go to the top of it so we climbed up and it was so pretty from up there! The sky was orange and all we could see from up there were buildings, but still it was very pretty and we were just talking and at that moment I actually felt like I could trust him with anything. We were talking about our most embarrassing moments and his was when he dumped Reena and when she told few people that he used to sing for her and she took a video of it once and she sent that video to all his friends. Later they had a big fight and everyone just forgot about that video slowly. And I said "You sang for her?" and he blushed a little and said "I was pretty cheesy last year…but well…YouTube loved me…" and I just laughed and he said "But that was last year… I am not that cheesy anymore…is that a good thing?" and I said "If you ask me then yes it is a good thing but few girls like too cheesy…. So I don't know" and he just said "Hmm…." And then he asked me for my most embarrassing moments and for some reason I could not think of any. I am still not sure if it took me so much time to think of one embarrassing moment because there were none or because there were so many…. Probably the latter one. I remember when I went to my family friend's beach house once and few people were serving food around the pool and I was trying to push my friend into the pool so I pushed her and she caught onto my hand while she was falling and we fell on one of the people who were serving and that person fell into the pool along with both of us and the tray of food he was serving. That was pretty embarrassing. I told Akarsh about this and he laughed and I just said "Shut up!" and later when we were talking he asked me "So.... You and Jai... Are you guys like...a couple?" and I said "What? No.... we are just best friends. That's all. Who told you that we were a couple?" and he said "No one came and told me but Rajesh was talking to me in the second week after I joined school, we were talking about something when he suddenly asked me if I liked you and I was just going to reply when he told that he was asking because Jai and you are a couple and that I shouldn't really interfere. And then few guys around him laughed and so did he, but I didn't know if he was kidding or if he was serious" I said "Don't ever listen to a word Rajesh says. He's just one of those annoying guys who don't have a life of their own." and Akarsh just gave me this big smile so I asked him what that was supposed to mean but he just said "Nothing... Shall we leave? It's getting pretty late" and I said okay and we left. The whole time all I wanted to know was what that smile meant. But why did I care so much? It was just a smile...right?

Chapter 8

Naina did not come to school today and Aaliya was with Tina as usual and she just said "Hi" to me once in the morning and sat next to Gia in class. I was sitting behind Jai and Raj who sit together every day and Akarsh sat behind Raj and to my left. Raj, Jai, Akarsh, and Sam have become pretty close, Rohan started coming to school only after the first month since he went to the United States for his cousin's wedding. It was such a shock for him to see what had happened between Tina and me. He is not that close to Akarsh as the other guys, but they are okay. The guys started talking to Akarsh when he started basketball coaching since Jai and Sam go for that too, they played together after class and then somehow they just became friends and he played football with the other guys at break once and Raj slowly started talking to him. Now they have inside jokes and actually understand each other. I slowly started getting okay with the fact of not being Tina's friend since it did not really make such a big difference to me anymore. The only reason I was worried was because I did not want the group to split and we did not exactly split….I guess you figure out who your actual friends are at times like this and yes it hurts me but I guess it is just what was meant to happen. Tina was not that close to Jai or Sam and they had their own reasons not to like her and for some reason and Raj is talking to her normally like how Aaliya is talking to me nowadays or maybe a little more than that and Rohan is talking to Tina and me both like he always used to.

The only problem is that Tina is telling Aaliya something about me and she tends to believe it, she is not close to me anymore and she was my best friend. While I was thinking about all of this, Kayla came up to me and asked if she could sit in the empty seat to my right and I told her that she did not have to ask me and that she could sit if she wanted to, then Kayla smiled and sat. Our physics teacher came in and started talking to us about Newton's three laws in detail and then when the bell rang she said that she was going to separate us into few groups in the next class and that we were going to have an assignment on this chapter. After that we had two periods of math and half of the class was irritated as the first period of it got over. At break, I was with Aryan and Meera. Later we had physics period and during that class our teacher separated us into few groups. She asked us first, who wanted to be team captains and few hands shot up including mine. Aaliya also raised her hand. So the teacher chose four captains: Amar (one of the brainiest students in our class), Aaliya, Gia, and me. Even though Gia is very silent she likes assignments for some reason and so I think she just raised her hand when she heard that this was an assignment. Since there were twenty-four students in the class, each team had to consist of six students including the captain. But we did not get to choose who we wanted in the team. The teacher picked it. In my team I had Kayla, Akarsh, Raj, Rajesh, and Pooja. Pooja is pretty smart, but she is known better because of her super neat and organized projects and assignments. It was as though she hired a professional to do her stuff. I was very happy with my team actually. Except for the fact that Rajesh is really annoying and would not move an inch for this project and that since Kayla is there in the team, Raj will be flirting with her or trying to show off. Other than that I like my team.

The assignment was to make a small model or presentation that applies to any one of Newton's three laws of motion. And the submission was due two weeks later. So we all sat together and discussed about where to meet and do the project and who would bring what and do what. There was a hushed buzz in the air and soon we all started delegation duties. But we did not discuss the most important thing: which of Newton's three laws were we going to do, but we were going to discuss that later. We decided that we would meet at Kayla's place two days later and start working on the project. Just as we were talking, our English teacher called me outside the class to talk to me. She told me "Alisha, I heard that you acted in last year's play and that you helped a lot in shortening the script last year and helping the teachers and students out. So I was wondering if you would like to write a small script for short play that each team is supposed to do this year. As you know I am the head teacher of Ruby and I wanted to know if you wanted to try writing the script. Even few others are trying. You can submit it to me any time before the end of this month?" and I said "Yes ma'am, surely! I would love to" and she said "Good…it can be from three particular topics which I will tell you about later…let it just be short but don't worry if it is a little long…. Once you write the script we can make it shorter if we like. I just want you to create a basic story" I just nodded and then she told me to go back to class. To be honest with all the things happening between Tina and me I did not like school as much as I did before because Aaliya, my best friend did not talk to me anymore, the group does not talk as much as we used to before. And because Raj talks to Tina at times he tells me that she is not exactly upset but just does not talk about me and if she does then it is always like I am the bad guy. Many things have changed and for some reason I could not talk to Aryan in front of Tina anymore, it just felt a little uncomfortable. And so I found school very boring and I started getting irritated easily nowadays. I know it is not a big deal but I have never fought that much with a person who was once a very close friend ever before so it was different for me. I try protecting relationships and usually my fights or arguments with anyone from our group did not last more than three days at most. Change does not suit me and so school did not seem that interesting anymore. So when ma'am told me about the small play and asked me to write the script I was happy since writing is one of the things I love and would take my mind of these small stupid issues for a while. Later when I went home I called Naina and she told me that she would not be coming to school for maybe a few weeks since her cousin suddenly called her parents the previous night and told them that her granddad's condition was pretty serious and that he wanted to meet them as soon as possible. I just told her to take care and hung up. I could not help being a little selfish and think about what I would do in school when Naina is not there. Just then I heard a cycle bell from outside and since I was standing next to my window I looked down and Akarsh was standing there and I smiled and waved. He waved back and asked me to come down so I changed and went down, took my cycle and both of us went cycling. After about twenty minutes, we went to the place we go to most of the time, his house terrace. We got two ice cream sticks before going and were talking. I started talking about how Naina was not going to be there in school and that the guys would talk but at break they usually go for football and that Tina and Aaliya are going to act super weird as usual. I do not want Aaliya to get hurt because Tina talks to Aaliya properly but talks behind her back and Aaliya tells Tina everything and Tina tells all of that to her other friends and says that Aaliya has such stupid issues to deal with. I told Akarsh "You know what? Sometimes I just wish that I could rewind my life and sort things out" and he said "Everyone does..." and I said "I could still run away, you know? To New York or London or Italy" and he just laughed and said "Yeah...you could do that...but then what about everyone here who care for you..." and I said "Like who? Tina is now a stranger and Aaliya isn't on my side when I need her and Naina isn't picking sides but for some reason I feel like nowadays she is also drifting apart. The guys are just neutral and they think this is a very small issue and it is but I am hurt that the people who I used to trust so much and the people who I care about so much aren't there for me anymore, it's like everyone just left me and moved on..." And he said "What about me? I am not going anywhere..." and I just smiled at him. Akarsh just knows when I need him to kid around and when I need him to listen and help me.... And he understands me better than anyone else. We were silent for some time after that for no reason. We were just engrossed in staring into outer space and thinking about different things. Suddenly I could feel his palm touching mine. It was warm and it was like his gesture or way of saying that he was there for me. I did not mind him holding my hand either. We just went on talking and then we had to leave so I cycled back home and started doing my homework. Every night before sleeping, when I close my eyes, I always think of the things that I feel happy about or things that I wish happen and today all I could think of was Akarsh. I have gotten really close to him and for some reason I really like him, maybe even more than a friend. I smiled to myself for some reason and dozed off. It was a Friday the next day and it was also my uncle's birthday so my mom had organized a surprise party for him and called all our close friends for dinner that night. And school was not that awkward because every time Tina and Aaliya walked by me I just did not seem to notice or care about them. I was talking to Kayla the whole day and we had lunch together and we actually are very alike. Akarsh and I were talking in class when Tina came in and started talking about Aaliya and me to Gia. Tina started talking to Gia a week ago and she thought that they were pretty close, but Gia was just new and shy so she just listened to everything Tina said and nodded and gave an innocent smile. I could hear what Tina was talking about clearly but acted like she did not know that, I'm pretty sure that she wanted me to hear whatever. At one point she looked at Akarsh and me and turned to Gia and said "First it was Jai then Aryan and now it's that new guy…poor guy, he doesn't know who she really is" I was really upset when she said this but just forced myself to shut up but Akarsh just stood up and pulled me by my hand and started walking off and when he passed by Tina he just said "I understand that you are attention seeking and having people talk about you makes you happy and that you want us to listen to whatever you say but just try being a little more subtle the next time?" Tina did not even say anything, for the first time ever because usually she has some stupid reply for everything so this time she just walked out of class. I just laughed when Akarsh and I got out of class and asked him "What was that all about?" and he said "Nothing….I don't even know where that came from but she was pretty annoying and was repeating the same thing again and again so…yeah. Someone had to do it."

Later that day my group decided to meet at Kayla's place this weekend to start our project since it was due next week and we had to start. We finally decided that we would do the third law of motion by Newton for our project, every action has an equal and opposite reaction. We decided to make something like Newton's Cradle to demonstrate the law and we were also going to make two charts, one talking about Newton and one explain about the law. On Saturday, we all started working on whatever we were assigned at Kayla's place and to my surprise we got a lot of work done. When Kayla was talking to her mom, Akarsh came and sat next to me. I was doing a little design for the borders of the chart and every time I make the borders for a chart I become so nervous as though if I mess that up then every single thing is ruined and the one thing I always worry about is if it is in a straight line or not. I was busy doing the border so I did not really realize who was sitting next to me. I finally finished one part of it and moved away from the chart to see how it looks when Akarsh said "It's fine! Calm down" and I just smiled and nodded. And he said "Hmm… I wanted to talk to you…" and I said "Yeah?" and he said "After we finish the project?" and I just nodded and he went to Raj. Akarsh has been acting quite strange for some reason… and I really wanted him to stop because it was scaring me. I didn't understand why but when he was going to talk to me today I decided that I would ask him. After the project work was over we were all going to leave and by the time I went to Kayla's room to get my stuff and came back Akarsh was gone…apparently his dad came to pick him up. Now how was I going to talk to him?

Chapter 9

Akarsh called me that evening and was talking about general stuff and that is when I asked him why he was acting so strange lately. He told me that he was not and that he had to go because his mom was calling him and so I said bye and he cut the call. I did not like where this was heading…we were so close and suddenly it feels like he is avoiding me for no reason…the only thing I could do now was confront him in school tomorrow. Sometimes I feel that Akarsh acts like such a girl…like a girl on her periods actually… He gets so moody and starts over thinking about every single thing! He is actually worse than me in these "phases" he goes through. But I was not going to break my mind over this.

So I then went to sit and do my homework when I remembered about the play-writing thing that ma'am asked me to do. I decided that since I finished my homework I would sit and think of few ideas for the play. Ma'am said that it could be anything as long as it's quite short and "to the point." Later that day, ma'am also told me that it should make a statement or create awareness and that our school has taken up three topics:

1. Do not drink and drive.
2. Recycling.
3. The negative points of education.

Out of the ten people who were working for the short play from our school, four already chose "Do not drink and drive" and three chose "Recycling" so I thought that I would do a play on "The negative points of education." Yes it is accepted that education is very essential for our lives, but few people take it way too seriously and get hurt in the bargain. Education is something that is given to a person to improve their standards of living and provide them with better life, wisdom, and knowledge, but when a kid faces hard times in our education systems due to the grades he/she get in examinations or because the individual is not very book smart and when the system makes us feel like the problem is actually within ourselves then it ruins the kid, he will lose his confidence and happiness and will feel unwanted. For all this not to happen, we need proper educationalists that can guide children and help them in such times of confusion. Children are all good in something or the other, maybe one child is good in studies whereas the other is in sports, but when few people compare the two kids in the studies aspect, one will seem to be more superior and hence will be seen in a different light. Few kids are mature and strong enough to understand that people are going to say things and comment but letting it affect his/her self-confidence is not right. But most kids get affected when people start comparing them and will try so hard to achieve in area that are of no interest to them and end up leaving their talents behind. Our society has a way of believing that only kids who get good grades are considered smart, which is so untrue. There are kids who are very book smart and hence get amazing grades but are not very street smart so suffer when it comes to actually working in the real world. Kids who have been put down for most their lives and who have been called dumb or stupid are the ones who make it big at times because they do their best to hone their skills and fight all the criticism and insults to show everyone what they are capable of but some are not strong enough to face all that people throw at them. Some form a bubble around themselves and start believing that they are not special and are just average. This isn't right, is it? I even clearly remember this one time when I was ten years old and I had gone to my family friend's house and our parents were talking when the little girl who was about my age came running into the room with a huge smile on her face and her test book in her hand and screamed "I got full marks in my science test!" and her mom said "Very good darling! Now go change and come we are going out for lunch" and after the kid left the room literally jumping with joy her mother told my mom "She is really good in science. I am sure that she is going to be an engineer when she grows older. I even started talking her into it. What is your daughter going to do?" and since I was ten I really had no clue. All I wanted was to excel in whatever I liked and did and be happy. I was feeling weird, uncomfortable, as though I was being judged and so my face drooped down and I did not say anything. Noticing this my mom instantly said "She is good in so many things that is hard to choose one career path…once she is older and has a little more knowledge I will sit with her and discuss and provide her with everything she needs to achieve her goals. I think that's fair." And the other lady just smiled and nodded. I do not even know if it meant anything to her but it meant a lot to me! For me to know that my mom supports me and sensible people understand me was much more important than one stranger. Do not get me wrong, I know that there are a million people who must be having the exact same mind-set as the lady I met and I do not mean her any harm, but sometimes they talk without thinking and I do not know what I would have felt if my mom did not say whatever she said, it made all the difference and actually gave me the confidence in everything I do. Yes at times I do have stress due to studies but then again, who does not? Any teenager reading this now and saying "oh I don't!" is just not to be trusted. Anyway I am just drifting away from the topic in hand, how should the play be? Since I have chosen education I decided to make it about how the education system can make or break us and about how the choice is actually in our hands. I decided to make it a story about how there are two best friend, names unknown at this moment, and how they shift schools in the twelfth grade which is a pretty important year for senior school. Both these boys are very alike and they are very good in the academic aspect too. Along with the peer pressure and the need to make new friends, they struggle to get used to the pattern of teaching. The teachers do not help them as much as they need and so the night before the exams when one of the boys was studying he could not take it anymore: the stress of making his teachers happy, the pressure of making his parents proud, proving himself to everyone.

He then writes his exams and when he gets his final grades that make or break his entry into his desired college, he sees that the grades are average and do not meet the cut off. In the quick second of not knowing how to show up in front of his parents, he thinks that there are only two solutions to his situation: running away or committing suicide. However drastic it may seem, for a pressurized mind at the very moment when every thought add every second is racing in your brain, thoughts like this pop in. He did not know where to run so he chose the latter option and that was the biggest mistake. But just by saying that it was his mistake to commit suicide we are not changing a thing, did anyone even wonder why he chose such a horrible choice of ending his life? No one chooses it that easily right? Did anyone think of it in his point of view? Was there anyone to help him when he needed help? All these questions have just one answer. No. The other boy suffered equally as the one that committed suicide, but he did not give up that easily because he had understanding parents who helped him through his stress and he understood that trying his best is all that he can do too. He did not let the education system overpower him, he studied as much as he could and wrote his exams well. I am not going to exaggerate by saying that he topped his class but yes he did considerably well. Through the play you can basically show two students who were very alike but differed due to the kind of support they received and the mind-set they had. How grades are all that matter nowadays and people go through any kind of trouble and sometimes even choose a wrong path to get them. As a child I would have never thought that a few alphabets would rule over my life and set my future but well, here we are. Nowadays credit for talent is nothing if you have not got a certificate and marks to prove it. Smartness is judged with how well you by-heart things in a book and spill it on paper, and in most subjects, we are not even allowed to interpret things as we understand them, we need to answer it word-to-word as given in the textbooks. Now how is that going to help me in the future? How does that teach me hard work or practical thinking? I actually thought that this would be a good way to voice my opinions and so I went with this idea and before starting executing it, I wanted to run this by my teacher and so I decided that I would meet her in school the next day...hopefully she likes it. I was then thinking about something few teachers announced in school...they said that the people representing the school in the short film competition get to go to Delhi to participate if their idea gets chosen and now I actually got even more excited than I already was about this competition. Well that thought went away from my mind when Akarsh sent me a message saying "hi." I was not going to reply because I know that if I bring up the question of why he is ignoring me he would change the topic completely so I just did not say anything at all. The next day the first thing I did when I saw Akarsh was stop him from going anywhere, made him sit down and spoke to him about this. Obviously, he kept saying that he was just upset about something that happened at home and that it had nothing to do with me and usually I would have bought something like that but I just felt like he was hiding something for some weird reason. Before I could say anything Ron just runs into class and pulls Akarsh by saying "Leave your girlfriend alone for two minutes at least! The bus is going to leave soon and you don't want to be late for your first football match from this school. Now come!" and the weird thing is that neither Akarsh nor I denied the fact that I was his girlfriend or said anything to Ron for that reason. I just screamed "Best of luck you idiots!" As they left the room, Kayla came in and sat next to me and nowadays Kayla and I have gotten really close. Naina came back to school a week ago…weird that I did not mention her? Well…she has not exactly been worth mentioning. I called her five times when she was away just to find out how she was but she did not pick up even once. I thought she was busy so I left it but apparently she spoke to Tina, Aaliya, and Jai but not me for some reason. She was ignoring me in school and was with Tina and Aaliya the whole time. And if this happened before then I would have been so interested in finding out what was going on but now I was just not bothered anymore. I figured that Aaliya and Tina must have said something and she would have believed them or she just feels like if she is going to stick with me then she will lose their friendship since it will seem like she is pickings sides. Either way Naina was not talking to me anymore. Everything was not going as I planned at all.... tenth was supposed to be a perfect year, a year filled with surprises. But when I said surprises I did not exactly have this in mind. Things were changing too much too soon and I was not comfortable with it at all. I kept telling myself that I was alright but no... I was not. They were my "best friends" and they hence do not just get to leave me behind and move on. It was so unfair but then again life isn't fair. I was talking to Kayla nowadays about everything. We had become really close so soon and she was always there through my ups and downs. I thought it would be best not to give our relationship a name. Friend, true friend, best friend...too many options you see. Labels are for jars, not for relationships. The same applied when it came to Akarsh. Best friend, crush, whatever. Kayla came in and the first thing she asked was "So...you and Akarsh eh?" and I just said "What? No...we're just friends and you know that" and she said "Well then someone should really explain that to both of you because when you guys are together you can't stop smiling and blushing" and immediately I responded by saying "I don't blush!" and she said "Oh...you most definitely blush... I will take a picture the next time and show you" and I just rolled my eyes playfully and we were interrupted by the teacher rushing into class since she was late.

Chapter 10

Well Kayla kept her word and actually took a picture of Akarsh and I when we were talking in her house one day before the project was due. And after seeing the picture I understood why few people would mistake us for a couple. The picture was taken when I was cutting some paper and he was writing on the chart, when he was trying to make me write so that he would get to do the easier job of cutting pictures to stick on the chart. I did not let him so he started playfully fighting with me for the scissors. Yes that sounds dangerous but that is not the point here. In the picture, I was standing and his hands were wrapped around me from behind and he was trying to snatch the scissors and both of us were laughing. The picture was really cute and yes, Kayla was right. As much as I hate admitting it, I was blushing but I was not going to accept that so I just said that it was the lighting that made me look like that. Akarsh and I were like a couple in few ways I guess, we have pointless arguments about the smallest things, talk about things we have not shared with anyone else and hold hands at times. But to my defense, we only held hands when it was necessary: when one of us was talking about something really emotional and sad or something. It was a symbolic gesture of saying that we were there for each other. He made me happy…he made me blush! No one has ever made me feel the way I did right now but I did not know what these feelings meant, I was new to these feelings. I have had crushes before but they have not lasted this long and I was never this close to a guy I had a crush on. But with Akarsh, it is just so different. It is like taking a baby and placing the baby in a room full of lights and rainbows, mirrors, and sunshine…the fascination, confusion, and happiness experienced by the baby would be explain exactly what I was going through now. I was not going to talk about this to anyone though…may this just be within and no one needed to know. Well Kayla was not going to let it be that way. That night it was 9 pm by the time all of us finished and packed up. My parents usually do not let me sleepover in houses where they do not know the family, but since they have met Kayla's parents, they were fine with me sleeping over there as it was also getting too late and I had school the next day. My mom sent me my clothes, toilet kit, and my school bag for the next day. That night when I was texting Akarsh, it was different. Both of us were sort of flirting. I am new to flirting as well. Each word we said just sounded so… so…flirtatious! And the weird thing was that I did not even realize. It seemed like a normal conversation to me and I did not think twice before I replied and somehow it just felt like normal conversation but when Kayla read a few messages she pointed out the obvious. Kayla forced me to put my mobile phone down and told me that it was pretty evident that Akarsh and I liked each other and I kept denying it for some time but its Kayla…she knows how to get what she wants very slyly. She got it out of me… I said it… I told her everything that I felt. And she was smiling and literally jumping on the bed and said what I knew she would say: "I knew it!" I started laughing and said that I did not want to talk about it anymore and there we ended that conversation, but I have to accept that I was happy talking to someone else about what I feel, someone I could relate to, someone who understood me and did not expect anything from me.

That night I slept off soon...thinking about the past, thinking about how everything happens for a reason. Soon I woke up to the alarm ringing at 6 am. Kayla was silently snoring and I had to hit her with a pillow to wake her up. She groaned when the soft blue pillow hit her face and slowly stretched out and woke up. We played stone–paper–scissors to decide who would take a bath first and since I won, she went in first. As a reflex action, I checked my mobile phone and found a message from Akarsh that was sent just ten minutes ago.

Akarsh: Rise And Shine Al :*

Akarsh: Shit! Sorry I meant :) not :*

Me: I liked the first message better...

Akarsh: Me too...

And that was enough...Enough to make me smile and make me feel all warm and happy. Kayla just then walked out of the bathroom with a towel on her shoulder and when she saw me smiling she pulled my mobile phone and read the message and started smiling too. And then she threw my mobile phone back at me and went to take her clothes. I asked her "What?" and she said "nothing" and continued smiling and I said "Just say it" and she asked "Say what?" and I said "What you are holding yourself back from saying" and she laughed and said "I was just thinking about how you guys have already started the 'good morning' messages... nice waking up to one of those isn't it?" and I had to accept, it did feel really good but I just threw a pillow at her and went into the bathroom to get ready.

At school Akarsh and I were not awkward at all...we did not talk about the message, but it was evident that both of us were happy getting our feelings slowly out in the open.

We were talking about music covers because Akarsh plays the guitar and the piano and I sing and we just thought that if we made covers and posted them on Facebook or YouTube, it would be fun. That evening Akarsh invited me over to try to practice for the music covers and I said that I would ask my mom and come. My mom was okay with it as long as I came back home by 7:30 pm and I left at 4 pm so it was not a problem. Akarsh's mom answered the door and said "You must be Alisha… I have heard so much about you" and I just smiled and started talking to aunty until Akarsh came down. Aunty was really sweet and I tend to talk quite a bit to mothers and try to make a good impression because I like it when people like me. Anyway Akarsh came down and told his mom that she could have me later and that now we were going to go practice in the TV room. His mother said that she was going to the grocery store and that she would be back soon. I was confused as to why we were going to the TV room but understood when I saw the room. There was a piano that was red and beautiful! It looked especially pretty in this room, it looked so classy and amazing. I love the piano…I have been learning for the past three years. As soon as I saw the piano, I just started walking towards it and sat down and started playing a few notes. Akarsh sat down next me and asked "You play?" and I nodded saying yes. And then I said "I have always wanted a red piano… I love how it looks. My parents think that the black piano is the only one that goes with our interior but this piano… it's just so…beautiful!" and just then I started to play the song "If I Lose Myself" on the piano and without asking any question Akarsh started playing it on the guitar as well and I started singing and in few parts he joined me in singing and this sounded beautiful. The piano and the guitar sounded magical together but the thing that impressed me the most was the fact that Akarsh's voice along with mine sounded so good. I loved singing with him, and as soon as we finished, he placed the guitar next to the wall and sat back next to me. He said "That sounded really good" and I looked at him and said "I know. We should do this more often!" and he just kept staring and I asked him "what?" and he said "Nothing, you're just…different" and I said "Different good or different bad?" and he instantly said "Different good. Definitely good" and I just started saying "Oh then…" and he leaned in and kissed me. It was a quick small soft kiss but…it was my first. In that kiss that lasted for not more than a few seconds I could feel his breath, his warmth and my stomach did a back flip…my mind went blank. As soon as he moved back both of us looked equally surprised. I was surprised that he kissed me and I guess he was too. The room that was once filled with music just a few minutes ago now was quiet. There was not a single noise and we just sat there. We looked at each other for a minute after we kissed but then turned away after that single minute. Then he interrupted the awkward silence by saying "I am not going to apologize for doing that Al… I have been waiting to do that from the time I saw you" and I just nodded and he said "Well…please say something!" and I just blurted out the first thing that came to my mind "That was my…um…first kiss" and he smiled and scratched his head and said "Um…mine too."

Chapter 11

I couldn't stop thinking about him! Akarsh was running through my mind the whole night and I was confused as to how this was going to change our relationship and I did not what to do…as soon as I ate dinner I went up to my room with Tiara following me, and when I lied down on my bed Tiara slept next to me on the bed and I kept stroking and checked my mobile phone and found a message from Akarsh;

Akarsh: Hey

Me: Hi

Akarsh: About today…

Me: If you want to act like it never happened I get it

Akarsh: Are you kidding? Why would I want to act like it never happened? Al… I really like you.

Me: Me too, But…

Akarsh: It's okay…. I am willing to wait until you are ready to give 'us' a chance. You just have to tell me when you are Al

With that one message I went to sleep, I was confused, happy, and feeling loved all at the same time. I could not stop thinking about the kiss and about how I wanted to experience it all over again.

The next day was normal surprisingly, I thought Akarsh would be all weird around me again but he seemed pretty alright. He was the same best friend that he was just two days ago. Kayla seems to know me too well and came to me and asked "How was the music covers thing with lover boy?" and I said "The covers were really good...and don't call him lover boy" Kayla just said "Actually...what happened after the music covers thing?" and I said "Nothing. I went home..." and Kayla said "Oh come on Al! I know you better than that...what happened between the both of you?" and I made her swear that she wouldn't open her mouth about it to anyone including me about this later and told her in detail about every single thing that happened the previous evening: the music, the cover, the kiss, and the texts. Kayla's smile was just widening detail by detail and at the end the only thing she had to say was "Whoa Whoa I didn't know lover boy was such a romantic" and I just rolled my eyes and told her not to talk about it anymore, but Kayla just broke her promise by talking to me about it again and asked me how it made me feel and questioned me so much. I do not know if it was the kiss or the talk with Kayla, but I seemed to fall for Akarsh more day by day. His smile, the way he gets me, his voice...and not to mention...his good looks. But I locked these feelings inside me until I was sure about my feelings...like 100% sure!

Oh God! He makes it so hard for me to lock my feelings for him! He puts in so much of an effort just to talk to me and be with me and even though we aren't exactly in a relationship, I just want to hold his hand and be in his arms all the time but obviously that would ruin our friendship so I left it.... And that's when the incident happened. The incident that kind of changed things. From the time I started getting close to Akarsh, I drifted away from Aryan and I guess since he is not in my grade either we did not even see each other often. This went on for some time and slowly Aryan and I almost felt like we were not a part of each other's lives. One day, few of us were asked to stay back after school to discuss on who would be going to Delhi for the short film festival and who would stay back. I had no idea who else from our school was selected for it, but I would get to find out soon. Just then when I walked into the room no one was there and hence I decided to wait… I was looking at all the chart papers put up in the class and that's when I heard someone's footsteps behind me. It was Aryan and for a minute there was this awkward silence in the room but then I said "Hey… How come you're here?" and he said "Oh… Hmm… I just saw the classroom open and wanted to check if someone was inside before I closed it from the outside… Long time since we spoke huh?" and I simply nodded and he started briefing me about all that I had missed in the past two months. I mean obviously I heard about him from others but did not have a proper conversation with Aryan for the past two whole months. As we were talking, he told me that he was dating two girls at the same time and that he was doing amazingly well in studies too and was bragging about how perfectly fine he was. This was something I found weird because Aryan was never "that" guy: The guy who thinks he is so perfect and brags about girls that fall for him. Aryan had changed, in almost two to three months he had become a guy I did not know anymore. A guy who dated girls for the action and later dumped them when they seemed boring. A guy who spoke only about himself and was the least bit bothered about anyone or anything else.

The guy who thinks that the world runs on his say. He became THAT GUY. I was trying to talk about things that we used to so that he would act normal again and not put up this fake "cool guy" attitude, but he acted like he did not remember any of our inside jokes anymore, and for all

I know he genuinely forgot about them. And the weirdest thing is that he was flirting with me. I know guys flirt… But there are these few guys who you can never flirt with, guys who are never going to be more than just friends…. Guys that you "Friend-zone" and that's who Aryan was for me: The guy I have NEVER pictured dating and I thought he felt the same way so it was really awkward and weird when he tried to inch his way out of the friend-zone. And as he was talking, he slowly came next to me, sat down, and held my hand. I moved my hand away and said "Aryan… I don't want to be giving you the wrong signals here but we are just friends…that's all" and he said "This is all because of this Akarsh guy isn't it? I heard you guys are getting very friendly…really Alisha? You guys are such good friends that I don't even exist in your life anymore?" and I just stood there, not knowing how to reply. I never knew Aryan felt insecure, I still considered him as a really good friend. Accepted that we were not as close as we were before but that did not mean he was not a part of my life anymore. I started to explain when he said "And don't tell me you never had feelings for me… So many people came and told me that you did and slowly I started developing feelings for you. Then all of a sudden you just move on to another guy? So what? You're just a tease?" and I said "Excuse me? Aryan you were ALWAYS just a friend. And since when did you start believing rumors? We were always really good friends. That's all. Don't try to bring Akarsh into this" and he said "Oh now you are defending him too huh? Nice okay." And he just moved so close to me that we were just a few inches apart when he said "You have to choose. It's either me… or him" and I just said "What is the matter with you? You sound like you just jumped out of a movie! Stop making everything so very dramatic…It feels like I don't even know you anymore…" and just then Akarsh entered the class, he saw Aryan standing inches away from me and I could just see the irritation in his eyes. Aryan laughed and said "Listen… Just leave us alone for some time? All this started only after you came into the picture anyway" and Akarsh just walked towards Aryan and said "So you are blaming me for Alisha's lack of feelings for you? Seriously? Why don't you just get the point already? She never was and still isn't interested in you" This was starting to become too big a scene for no reason but I did not know how to stop this either. Aryan then said "You think you know her so well, don't you? I have known her longer and know her better than you so why don't you just take a step back?" I could not believe how immature this argument was becoming. These guys who were both sixteen year olds, fought like they were five. I was going to tell Aryan to stop but Akarsh instantly replied saying "Time doesn't exactly define how well you know a person…. You might have a created more memories together but the feelings she has for me is the something that is not even close to what she feels for you." and Aryan replied saying "You aren't her boyfriend so just stay out of this and mind your own business…okay?" and Akarsh said "Ok you know what? Just stay away from Alisha okay?" And just as Aryan was about to take a swing at Akarsh, the other students walked by and peeped into the class and so Aryan just lowered his hand and said "Your school life is going to be hell as long as I am here" and walked away. The students ran away and Akarsh pulled me and we sat at the end of the class and he asked me about what had happened, I told him "It's nothing really. You don't have to even care about all this. It's not even that big of a deal" and Akarsh said "It's about you… Therefore whether it is small or big, I will care" and I know this sounds like such a cheesy line but when I saw Akarsh's eyes I understood that he actually meant it. That's when I was sure. Sure that I had feelings for him, sure that no other guy has made me feel this way and sure that I definitely was ready to give "us" a chance and could not hide my feelings anymore and so I said "God you make it so hard!" "So hard to what?" he asked with this confused expression on his face and I said "So hard to make myself hide my feelings for you" and he said "Wait…what? Did I hear you right? Did you just indirectly tell me that you have feelings for me?" and I said "I am not indirectly telling you anything. I am bluntly telling you the truth: I have feelings for you. I like you… A lot! So Akarsh Singh…. Would you want to maybe go out with me?" and he just said "Al! I was supposed to ask you that… You don't get to just ask me when I am about to ask you…" and I said "I don't 'get' to ask you? Why because I am the girl? You know what…" and with that Akarsh laughed and kissed me.

Chapter 12

Today was just so perfect. There is no other word that could describe today better than "perfect." Firstly, I accepted my feelings for Akarsh and now we are in a relationship and even though "being in a relationship" does not really change how we are around each other, it just makes me happy that even though I waited for fifteen years for my first relationship, Akarsh was worth the wait. Just seeing him makes me so happy and we are almost with each other throughout the day and it is like having a best friend and a boyfriend as the same person and that is just "perfect." That is not the only thing, we made rules. We decided that we would not be awkward around each other and we would not go publicize our relationship, of course we would tell our closest friends but after that if people get to know then alright but we would not go around telling people and making a big deal out of it because we would not want specific teachers finding out and blowing it out of proportion.

And this was not the only thing that made my day perfect. We found out that the people chosen for the short film competition were Piya, Siddarth, and Shania (three juniors who formed one team together for this competition); Tamara and Rahul (two seniors who were one grade above me), and Akarsh and I. We would be going to Delhi the next week and represent our school in the short film competition by presenting it to the judges at first and if selected we would get to submit it and the top three will be chosen from each age group and will be listed in the Best Junior Short Films of the year 2014 in India. Siddarth, Shania and Piya were representing for the age groups ten to thirteen; Akarsh and I for thirteen to sixteen; and Tamara and Rahul for sixteen to eighteen. We each got to choose not more than two other people to help us enact our characters in the short film. Akarsh too had submitted a different script, but ma'am chose my story and asked us to improve and present it together. We were all very excited and we had already chosen our two people for our play. Akarsh and I decided to take Kayla and Raj because they are two of the best actors we know from our grade and also because we were really close to them.

All this and the fact that Akarsh and I were finally together just made this day perfect. As soon as I reached home my mom asked me to help her set the table for dinner. I did just as she said with a smile on my face. Seeing this, she said "Well…someone looks extremely happy today… anything special happened?" and I just smiled and thought whether I should tell my mom about Akarsh. I mean, she already knows that he is my best friend and he has come home quite a few times and she talks to his mom and all so I guess it would not be such a big deal if I tell her. My mom and I share this relationship where I can tell her anything and everything that includes even things about crushes and relationships. So I said "Ma…. You know Akarsh, right?" and she looked at me and smiled and said "Yeah. Why?" and I said "Well I kind of like him and he kind of likes me too" and she said "And I kind of saw that coming… Now help me set this table."

Finally the day arrived. The day we all left to Delhi. My parents came to drop me off along with Kayla and they met

Akarsh there.... It was not the most awkward moment I have been in and at the same time not the most comfortable moment either. Akarsh was being so very formal and my dad was just being himself and joking around as usual. We were soon on the flight and I called dibs on the window seat and Akarsh instantly called dibs on the only seat that was next to the window seat. The teacher did not really have a problem with our seating arrangements as she was one of the few teachers in our schools who did not have a problem with stuff like this. Akarsh and I spoke for some time, but he was really sleepy and soon he dozed off. And I was listening to music with my earphones on and when I looked over at him I could not help myself from smiling, he was sleeping with his back straight, and I can never sleep like that! I just need to rest my head on something or someone. He also did not make a single noise when he slept, whereas my friends have recorded me sleep talking where it looks like I was talking to Channing Tatum and agreeing on marrying him (In my defense I had just watched "The Vow"). I continued listening to my music until I fell asleep. I had a feeling as though I was falling and woke up startled and that's when I realized that I had slept off with my head resting on Akarsh's shoulder and Akarsh had taken my earphones away without waking me up. This whole falling sensation that we feel in our sleep is something I have always wondered about. I read somewhere that there are different stories people believe, to explain this phenomenon. One of my favorite explanations was this: We can all agree that dying in your sleep is probably one of the most peaceful ways to die. People hence believe that angels come to carry us while we are asleep but sometimes these clumsy angels drop us and that's the falling sensation that we feel. However unreal that sounds, it is also the most creative way one could explain the falling sensation. Doctors explain that the jerk you wake up with is called a hypnic jerk to which the cause is still unknown. Anyway, let's get back to Akarsh… Shall we? He smiled at me and told me that I woke up right in time for landing and I told him that I was still sleepy and continued resting my head on his shoulder. I did not sleep though and Akarsh put one of his earphones on for me and we were listening to music. We soon landed at Delhi and it was 9 pm there, and by the time we got our stuff and went from the airport to the hotel, it was 10:30 pm. It was not as much of a hotel as it was a guest house; there was one room for the girls, one for the guys, and one for the two teachers who came with us. The guest house was actually well maintained and had cute balconies and I felt like this whole experience was going to be a lot of fun. I then went and opened our room balcony, held on to the fencing of the balcony and just stood out there, looking at all the lights that lit up the city at night. Just then when I looked to my right I saw Akarsh and he was lesser than an arm's distance away from me as all the balconies were connected. He was not looking at me, he was looking at the lights that I was admiring not so long ago and said "Even though the lights in New York are grander and the lights in Paris are prettier, the lights here have a very homely feel to them and just make you smile and stare… Don't you think?" and I just smiled at him and looked back at the lights…. Honestly, how many guys appreciate small details like lights and express themselves nowadays? Guys have this mentality of believing that when a guy says something sweet and cute or enjoys small pleasures like girls do then they are gay or they're weird. I so completely disagree. Guys have various fields to portray their masculinity in and when at times they express themselves; Girls don't find it weird…. We actually think that it's something unusual or different to find in a guy nowadays and get more attracted to that person. The fact that Akarsh could express himself so freely without thinking or caring about what others thought made me like him even more. I had never felt this way about a guy in my entire life and even though it was an amazing feeling, it was equally confusing for me. The next day we got to enact our play in front of the judges, and if we got selected, then we go through to the finals that would be two days later so we get one day in between to go sightseeing; and the fourth day, we all leave in the afternoon. Just as I was going through our plans for the next three days mentally, Akarsh slowly moved his palm over mine. His gentle touch just made me smile and I could just feel him looking over at me. I looked at him, still smiling, and he smiled back at me. We just stood there talking for some time and I told him that I had to go back in because the teachers would come for the final check-up before they go to sleep and he kissed me on my cheek and I went into my room.

Apparently, I was not the only one who was not sleeping; all the girls in our room were either listening to music or talking. One of the teachers came around for a final check to see if all of us were okay and then she went back to her room after checking the other rooms too. I changed into my pajamas and was talking to Kayla for some time. By 12 am everyone went to sleep, but I was still wide awake and so I went out to the balcony and shut the balcony door behind me so that none of the girls would be disturbed by the sound of midnight traffic. I started thinking about everything that was happening in my life. The fact that the few people who I thought were my best friends are not there for me anymore and about how now there are new people in my life that make me feel so special and about how I have learned to move on and accept reality and not crib about the past. As I was running through my past, I stumbled into the present: Akarsh. He made me feel like I was unique and made me feel like such a special person and that made me value myself more. He could see in me, things that I could not. According to him I was the prettiest, smartest, and most talented person. In his eyes, I was a figure of perfection and the things that I considered flaws, seemed to make me even better in his eyes. In his eyes, I was not the girl I thought I was. I wanted to know if I made him feel as happy as he made me and just when all these thoughts were going on in my head I heard the other balcony door open and out came Akarsh. As soon as he saw me he started laughing and said "You couldn't sleep either?" and I just smiled and said no. He jumped over the fenced partition between our balconies and sat down by me. I asked him whether all the guys had gone to sleep and he said that two of the guys were awake. We were just discussing about what we were going to do the next day when he said "Hmm… Al…" and I just looked at him and he asked "Would it be weird if I just put my… um…arm around you? I mean only if you don't mind" and I smiled and just nodded. I know that usually guys do not ask the girl's permission for stuff like this but I liked it when he wanted to know if I was okay with it. The inexperience that the both of us shared seemed to be oddly cute. He slowly put his arm around my shoulders and I just lay back on him and he kissed my forehead. We just sat there, me in his arms and him holding my hand. We spoke about the most random things that do not matter. Although we were talking about so many things, we were slowly starting to feel sleepy and we started blabbering, neither one of us paid attention to all of that because both of us were equally overwhelmed by that fact that we were together….Alone….Finally! This was all actually happening and was not just our imagination.

We were just talking about "The Catching Fire" movie and that is when he said "That scene in the woods when Peeta kissed Katniss.... There was no real emotion and it looked so very fake" and I said "Well how much more real could they make it seem? They're actors and however hard they try a kiss between two people who actually love each other will look different" and Akarsh said "So you're saying that if they actually loved each other then the kiss would have been better?" and I said "I guess.... Don't you think..." and before I could finish my sentence, Akarsh turned to me and so I turned to him and asked "What? What'd I say?" and he just kept looking at me and I could feel my heartbeat faster by the second and I did not know whether I had to lean in or what I had to do. Akarsh then leaned in and kissed me. This was not like the first time we kissed, this time it was a little more than just a peck, it was a little longer than the first time. When we came apart he just looked at me, we were staring into each other's eyes and did not speak a word. After a minute that felt like forever, he said "Now that's how a kiss should be" and he smiled and kissed me on my forehead and I laughed and lay back in his arms. Everything seemed so perfect and in his arms: I felt so protected, as though nothing could hurt me or bother me. We then almost slept off and when I suddenly woke up, Akarsh was already asleep. I woke him up and told him to go back into his room and sleep and that I would see him the next day. As I got into bed and was about to sleep I kept re-thinking about what had just happened a few seconds ago. Every second of it was replaying in my mind and I was smiling to myself and it was just a wonderful feeling. Yeah, that is the best way to describe it. It was a wonderful and magical feeling and all I wanted was for this to last a little longer.

Chapter 13

We are so nervous! We are all waiting in this small waiting room outside of the hall where we would have to go and enact our play. Akarsh and I managed to decide on the modified script but little did we know that acting what we created was not as easy as it seemed. All of us were rehearsing and were repeatedly correcting each other's lines even though we were not perfectly sure about our own dialogues. It was then time… time to go in and show the judges what we came here to do. It did not strike to me how hard it was and how much I wanted to win till this very point. I thought that since our script was good the play too ought to be good, but I was starting to feel like I must have miscalculated something. Before we entered we saw few of the other contestants and spoke about our scripts and it seemed like we were not the only ones with a good script. Hopefully we do well. With all of this running through my brain, our group got in with one of our teachers once the juniors group from our school came out. As soon as we went onstage, all I could see were all the people in the audience. Being in the school play is one thing, but representing your school in an all India event was something else altogether. I was scared about choking or falling off of stage… Basically, I was freaking out. We then acted out all that we had practiced and I realized that once I was on that stage, once I got into my character, I was not nervous anymore. I do not even know how I remembered all my lines; it was as though I was saying all of that from my very heart. Everything was going well until Raj forgot one of his dialogues… All of us did not even move from our places and even though we only paused for about two to three seconds, it seemed like a lifetime but all of a sudden Akarsh said something that was not even a part of the script and made it seem like that small pause was the thinking time the character he was playing needed before saying his dialogue in the play, and from, there we continued with the original script. As we came to the end of the play, we could hear loud cheers and applause from the judges and audience and that reassured me that we were not all that bad. As we got offstage, Raj started apologizing and all of us said that it was fine and that we were just happy that we are over with it now. That night when we reached the hotel all of us were exhausted, and as soon as we fell on our beds, we fell asleep. The next day I woke up at 6 am because I was hungry and my stomach was aching, and everybody else were sleeping because we were only going to go sightseeing and were going to leave only at 9:30 am. I was searching for food all around the room but could not find anything. Not even chips or biscuits. So I decided to do something that I didn't know if I should do: I went out to the balcony and jumped over the fence and into the balcony of the boy's room. Praying that most of them were at least half clothed I knocked on the glass door that was locked from the inside. All I could hear was moaning and some guy muttered saying "Someone go get that" and then it was all quiet again. I knocked again and that's when some guy kicked Rahul out of the bed who fell on Akarsh who was sleeping on the mattress, which was on the floor, and Akarsh just screamed. As both of them woke up, Rahul went towards the room's door and Akarsh came towards the balcony door. I could only see all of this through the translucent curtains.

Akarsh opened the curtains with his eyes squinting due to the sunlight and when he could properly see me he smiled and told Rahul to go back to sleep because it was me who was knocking. Rahul sighed and went back to his bed and fell asleep. Akarsh came out and shut the balcony behind him. He was wearing nothing but his boxers so as soon as he realized that and the fact that he had not brushed he ran back in and brushed quickly and got a T-shirt and came out. He asked me what I was doing there and I just told him that there was no food in our room and that I was starving and he said that they did not have any food either. I was so disappointed because my stomach was starting to growl and I really could not wait till 9 am for breakfast. Looking at me Akarsh said "okay see if you are really that hungry then there is this small bakery right outside the hotel which might be open at this time… We could come back before the teachers wake up" and I was so hungry that I accepted the offer and both of us decided to go. I was walking through the room and half the guys weren't even sleeping on the beds, they were sleeping in all possible places other than that. I almost tripped on Siddarth, but Akarsh held on to my hand and guided me through the room. Once we got out, we went down and carefully out of the hotel without the manager noticing and reached the little bakery that was close by. When I say bakery, I do not mean the cute ones that have pretty cupcakes and red velvet cake. I mean roadside Indian bakeries where you have to think twice before you choose something to eat if you have a sensitive stomach. I looked at everything and chose this tea cake and even though I insisted on paying Akarsh took my wallet away and paid for it which I later on forced him to share with me. We then were walking in the little garden of the hotel and eating. We were talking about the competition and laughing about how Rahul just forgot his dialogue and how Akarsh had to make up his own stuff to make it seem like it was planned that way. Later by around 8 am when we knew that the teachers were going to go to the rooms to wake everyone up, we quickly went upstairs. Right as we reached the rooms we saw the teacher leave hers and we did not want her to see the both of us exiting and elevator so Akarsh told me to go and ran into some room that was kept open because someone was cleaning it. I just calmly walked towards my room and when the teacher asked me where I was I simply said that I went down to the garden because I woke up very early and then she just asked me to go and get ready and told me that we would be leaving in an hour and a half. She then proceeded to the room where all the boys stayed so I was trying to come up with some idea to stop her from entering because Akarsh was not in there and so I just screamed when she was about to touch the doorknob saying "Ma'am!" and she looked at me startled and confused and said "What is it Alisha?" and I said "Hmm... Ma'am... Actually I was anyway going to the boys room to ask Siddarth for my charger so if you want I can tell them to get ready too" and she said "But I am already here...so I might as well just check on them. You can take your charger if you want to anyway" and I just nodded and waited anxiously as she slowly turned the doorknob.... I didn't know how she was going to react when she saw that Akarsh was missing... I remained in the corridor while the teacher walked in and after some time she said "Wait a minute.... Where's Akarsh?" and just then I was going to go to that unknown room that Akarsh was hiding in to call him but before I could do anything I heard Akarsh's voice from inside the boys room saying "Right here ma'am" and when I peeped in he was standing in the balcony. He must have come from the other balcony to this room as all the balconies are connected. That is one of the things I love about Akarsh. His presence of mind is so amazing that he can get out of any situation. I just laughed and went back into my room to get ready. As soon as I entered, Kayla came to me and pinched my arm and said "Where the hell were you? You got me worried sick, you know that?" and I was just rubbing the part that she pinched me and made a face at her and said "I wanted something to eat and there was nothing here so Akarsh took me to that small bakery outside and got me something" and Kayla said "Wait wait…. What'd you mean there was no food here? I have two cup noodles stuff in my bag…." And I said "Well how am I supposed to know? And all of you were asleep. I woke up at 6 am" and the Kayla said "He was awake too?" and I said "No… I kind of woke him up" and she said "How?" and I explained to her that I went into their balcony and told her about how all the guys were asleep and about how Rahul fell on Akarsh and also about how Akarsh came and opened the door for me and she said "Whoa whoa.. Hold it right there…you saw him in just his boxers?" and I just laughed and said "Kayla! Out of all that I said, that's the only thing that you got?" and she said "Just answer the question!" and I said "Yes…for like a second" and she just winked and laughed at me and I just rolled my eyes.

Chapter 14

Later we all got ready and got into the bus to go sightseeing.

I knew for a fact that Kayla was going to bring the fact that I saw Akarsh in his boxers up sometime during the day and I was right. Right before all of us got into the bus, Akarsh and I went towards this little coffee shop to get something to drink so before we left he asked Kayla what she wanted to which she first just replied saying that she did not want anything but then I saw it…that smile on Kayla's face. And right that instant I knew that she was going to bring up the incident that had occurred this morning… the question was: How? Just then Kayla said "Actually Akarsh…. I do want something. Just an answer to a simple question?" and Akarsh said "Hmm… Sure. What do you want to know?" and she said "I was just wondering if your boxers were striped or plaid…" and Akarsh, to my surprise, actually answered the question by thinking for a second and saying "Actually they were plain black…." Then he winked at me and asked "Right?"

The rest of the day was actually pretty amazing. I got to spend the whole day with him and my two best friends in Delhi. We were on the bus for the most part of the day where Akarsh and I sat together. I called shotgun for the window seat, and towards the end of the day, he let me stretch my legs out on his lap because my legs were hurting way too much. Our teachers got a call from the judges of the short film contest and they had told our teachers that Akarsh and I were selected for the next round and so did Tamara and Rahul, which meant that we got to stay in Delhi for two more days to shoot our short film and submit it to them. The juniors did not make it and hence one teacher was accompanying them back to Mumbai the next day. I had no idea as to how we were selected after the little mishap onstage but apparently it did not make a difference. That night we all went to attend a little dinner party organized by the Short Film Festival Group, where all the groups chosen for the next round would be present. We were all so excited and I was still in shock that we were chosen. All I knew was that we had to give our 100% to this short film now… no more places for mistakes. The dinner was organized very well; all the participants were given ID tags that gave the information about the person's name and from which school and city the student was from. The event gave us contestants a chance to bond with people of same wavelength and interests, which seemed like a very good idea.

That's when I met them… The group of students from HSC School in Bangalore. They were a group of four kids who were only taking part in the category for thirteen to sixteen year olds. Their name tags informed me that their names were Riya, Sadhana, Mathew, and Devansh. Riya came up to me with a warm smile and said "Hi! I am Riya and these are my teammates. We're from Bangalore. You guys acted really well yesterday" her group seemed to agree by nodding along, smiling and saying "Yes… Yes." I thanked them and called Akarsh, Kayla, and Raj and told them that their script was amazing too. It was also the same topic we had chosen and their play was really good too. Our two groups seemed to hit it off and so even after dinner was over all of us were chatting up in the hotel by the pool until we were called for. We spoke about our scripts and about the depth and meaning behind the scripts and so much more. I liked them a lot and it felt nice to meet new people who were so similar to us.

The next day all of us got ready really quick and went to the place where we had to shoot the whole movie in one shot properly. As we reached a little late, we got assigned as the third last group that would be able to take the video. This meant that we had to wait almost the whole day for our turn. We were allowed to sit in this little room next to the hall where everyone was shooting. This room had a glass wall that looked into that hall and the room we sat in was also soundproof so we got to see everything that the other groups were doing. We all thought that we would all just chill and watch the other plays for some time and practice later because we were done with our script and only needed a little practice before shooting the movie. Little did we know that we had a lot more work than we thought because the other participants stole our script. They copied our script completely and acted it out without changing even a bit of it. Who are these participants you wonder? HSC School from Bangalore… Our new friends.

Why would they do that? Did they have no script of their own already? I had so many unanswered questions in my head. I was so confused. Later after their act was over, they came up to us and spoke to us as though nothing was wrong. I was really upset so I walked away, but I could hear them trying to talk to my other teammates and I could not take it anymore so I went up to them and said "Are you guys for real? Am I the only one that saw what just happened? You guys stole our script! Our play! You don't get to come to us after that and smile and chat as though we are best friends." Riya then responded by saying "Calm down. It's a competition…nothing personal sweetie" I just went closer and looked her in the eyes and said "Never, ever call me sweetie."

Now we had a little more than two hours left for us to go up and shoot our play. The only problem seemed to be the fact that we did not have a script. If we used our original script now, it would seem like we are the ones that copied them. We spoke about this with our teacher and when she tried talking to the concerned authorities, all they said was that since we do not have any actual proof and since this will cause a huge problem and inconvenience for everyone, they would not be able to exactly help us. The only thing they could offer was pushing us to the last act, thereby giving us more time to come up with something. All of us were breaking our heads over what we were going to do; we could not just quit and go back home. We all decided that even if not an amazing play, we will put up something because when we have done so much to come till here, we could not just leave. This play thing might not seem like an amazing accomplishment, but once you have got to the point where you know that the chances of you winning are very high, it is hard to just let go. We wanted to give it our best shot and not return home without putting up a good fight. The question that remained was, how?

That is when Akarsh said this "What if we try my script?"

Akarsh and I had both presented the teachers with two different scripts and the teachers preferred mine but liked Akarsh's concept too. That is why they even let us work together. I had read bits of Akarsh's script and the base concept was the same with a few tweaks here and there.

If that school could steal our script and perfect in just one night then these few hours seemed enough for us to learn this. Akarsh came prepared with his script in his bag so we made a few copies of it and started rehearsing our roles in within half-an-hour. Since we were the last act now, we had two hours left until we go up and shoot so for one hour we all just practiced with the script and changed a few things to make this script work with the props and costumes we had for the previous script. The last hour was spent in seeing how everything fit and went along. This was not the best play, but it seemed good enough. Later one of the staff members came and called us in; we then stepped into the set and played our parts. Whenever one of us messed up a little, we got to re-take that part so that was playing to our advantage. Later after finishing the whole shoot, we all felt good about the fact that we at least tried and now even if we did not win, it did not matter. At least we gave it our best shot.

The teacher then took us all for ice cream because she thought we deserved it. We all went to a nearby ice cream shop and got our favorite flavors with whatever toppings. For some reason, we were all very quiet the whole time through. Through the silence, a wave of tension was shared by us all. We were all thinking about different things related to this one competition: Why did they steal our script? Why did they have to present our play? We could have won for sure if they hadn't done this! Was our other play good enough? Will we win something if not first place? God! I cannot wait for the results.

When we all were so deep in our thoughts, the teacher broke the silence by telling us that the results were going to be put up on the site in five minutes. That just made us even more nervous than we already were. So much was running through my mind and that is when Akarsh held my hand gently. He placed his palm over mine and just looked at me and that was enough to bring my heartbeat back to its normal pace. A few minutes later, we all took our mobile phones out to check the results and that is when we saw it: the rankings. We were in tie for third place with our best friends: HSC School, Bangalore. When we all read that, the first thing we did was laugh. The fact that HSC could not beat us even after their genius plans and the fact that we actually were the top three despite the last minute preparation made us feel so much better. We were all very happy with the results and started talking about how the one good thing that came out of all this, was that now we get to go back home with one hell of a story behind our great victory. We later went back to the place where the competition was held to receive our certificates and prizes. We were called up on stage along with HSV to receive our prizes, and the only difference between us two schools, was that we were so proud and happy, whereas they all just had an irritated look on all their faces. Third place had never felt this amazing before.

Chapter 15

It took a lot of effort for our teacher to get us back home the next day. We all did not want to get out of bed and leave this fun place and go back to tenth grade studies. Within these few days, we had all bonded and gotten closer. We all had such a great time and winning despite that tiny glitch in the end, just made us happier. I pulled myself out of bed to get ready first and once I was done, screamed for Kayla to go in. After changing into my clothes and packing my suitcase, I stepped out into that balcony for one last time. Seconds after I went into the balcony, Akarsh came into his. He laughed and said "This balcony is what I am going to miss most" and I nodded in agreement. The weather was so pleasant and there was a tiny continuous cool breeze hitting my face that felt so nice. As I looked into the garden of the guest house and the bakery next to it, I just smiled. Akarsh and I both just stood there and did not say a word because sometimes the silence is too perfect to be broken. Later the teacher came into our room and said that it was time to leave. It was actually hard for me to get out of the balcony knowing that I might never come back. Akarsh kissed my cheek before leaving and soon we were all on the bus on our way to the airport.

After reaching Mumbai, we all said our goodbyes and returned home with our families that came to pick us up. As we headed back home, I explained every tiny detail of the competition to my parents and about how we got third place despite all that happened. Hey! We overcame the whole cheating incident and won hence we get boasting rights. What is the point of it if you cannot exaggerate it a little and tell everyone? I knew that every car conversation at that moment was going to be only about this. I reached home to find the brownies my mother baked for me and she said that this was my reward for winning. And a reward it was, my mother's brownies are by far the softest brownies I have ever had and are a little gooey too. They have the perfect amount of chocolate, not too much, not too little, just right.

The remaining year of school was pretty good too. We all had a lot of studying to do, so the only thing that happened besides the studies was the school play where I played a little part, the music competition in which my group won second place, and a school carnival. Other than that Kayla and I got closer day by day and argued now and then for tiny issues but those would not last beyond one day. Kayla made me feel much more comfortable than Aaliya or Naina. We were so alike in so many ways and that just brought us closer. Naina and Aaliya came and apologized a little later when Tina had backstabbed them. They said that they just believed her and went along with whatever she said and did and regretted it and asked if I could forgive them. I was over all that happened and said that it was all in the past and I forgive them. I did actually forgive them. We did not go back to being as close as we were not just because of how they broke my trust but mostly because I had evolved a little from the girl I used to be. I wish I could say that Akarsh and I are still together, going to the same college and planning to get married, but that is not what exactly happened. We were together for a year and a half after which we just did not feel the same way about each other. We started arguing way more than usual and our feelings just seemed to deteriorate. Soon we grew apart and accepted that working on this relationship more that we already do did not seem to be the ideal solution and so we ended things before they got messier. Akarsh and I went through an awkward phase for about a month before we became friends again and right now he is one of my best friends. Kayla and Akarsh easily fall under the category of people who mean the most in my life now. Akarsh was my first boyfriend and I loved him. He was many of my "firsts" and he gave me one of the best years of my life. He actually continues to make me happy and understand me completely. The only difference is that he used to have the label of "boyfriend" before which has now gotten switched with that of "best friend." Thinking about all this brought a smile to my face and a tear to the eye. This is what high school was: crushes, haters, friends who stay with you till the end, friends who do not, acquaintances, people who study in your school but you do not talk to, guys who you like but are out of your league, guys who like you but you are out of their league, a guy who has the same feelings for you that you have for him, and those girls that understand you better than anyone else. All this mixed with some problems, mistakes, successes, inspiring people, irritating teachers, fun teachers, lot of studies, parties, movies, late night last minute studying sessions, tuitions, practice papers, and life lessons. You learn so much in high school that you might not learn anywhere else. Things in high school for some people can be hell, and for some, it can be okay. It has its own set of ups and downs but those will easily be the best years of your life. High school can either make you or break you…these are the years when we start making our own decisions. We have a mind of our own… How you handle situations creates you. Even if you make mistakes, which you will, learning from them is what is going to help you later. High school will not be like a bed of roses… You will be left heartbroken after break-ups, your crush may or may not like you back, you may get extremely low marks in a few tests, you will lose competitions, you will have blemishes, you will have days where you feel low for not one particular reason, you will have days when you think you look ugly, you will feel fat, you will feel weak, you will feel like running away from school and the people that hurt you, you will feel so much more. I know I have. But that's how you learn… Yes, you can learn from others mistakes too but when you get your fingers burnt is when you learn the hardest lessons. I wish I can tell you the cheats on how to avoid all this and just skip to the happy parts, but I cannot. No one can. Besides, if we never had lows then the ups would not even mean as much. You have to take every mistake as a lesson and never break down. To reach the top of the stairs, you need to keep moving forward regardless of how much your legs hurt. The same way, you have to keep moving on and moving over situations that hurt you to get to the top. Never lose hope and never ever stop dreaming. And if you do dare to dream, do not just stop there. Go forward and achieve that dream. Do everything in your power to get what you want if you see that 1% possibility of getting it. There will be people who break your trust, but those people should not be given so much importance. If you are going through something hard now, just know that things do get better. I am not just saying that… I mean it. I truly believe that this situation will turn around and you will smile again. When something ends, do not look at it as the end of everything. Think of it as a beginning of something greater. Some wise man said that "End is infinity. End without infinity is but a new beginning" and this is something I actually live by. Whenever you feel low or hurt, think about the people who make you smile, read something, go out somewhere, talk to someone, watch a movie, eat ice cream, open your own memory box, just do anything other than sitting in a corner and crying because that is going to take you nowhere. Just remember that things get better and life sure as hell goes on. No one has the right to hurt you and if they do, then be strong enough to not care. The more you care, the more authority you are placing in their hands. Life is too short to be lived with regrets, do what you think is right and deal with the consequences later. Stand up for what you believe in, always express yourself. Learn to say no when you do not really want to do something because peer pressure is something that is really easy to overcome if you do not give it that much importance. If people do not respect and love you for who you are, run away from them as fast as possible because they will change you and you are too perfect and unique to be changed. The only one that can mold or change you, should be you.

I need to go pack now because it is soon going to be time to step out of my little bubble and I need to go fully armed into the new battlefield; and by fully armed, I mean that I need to pack some family photos, cup noodles, and a teddy bear that I have had since the second grade.